W9-CPV-771

THE LOOP

THE LOOP
SHANDY LAWSON
HYPERION
NEW YORK

First Edition
1 3 5 7 9 10 8 6 4 2
V567-9638-5-13046

Printed in the United States of America

This book is set in Centaur MT.
Designed by Whitney Manger

Library of Congress Cataloging-in-Publication Data
Lawson, Shandy.
The loop/Shandy Lawson.—1st ed.
p. cm.
Summary: In New Orleans, Louisiana, star-crossed teens Ben and Maggie try to find a way to escape the time loop that always ends in their murder.
ISBN 978-1-4231-6089-2—ISBN 1-4231-6089-4
[1. Adventure and adventurers—Fiction. 2. Fate and fatalism—Fiction. 3. Murder—Fiction. 4. Death—Fiction. 5. Time—Fiction. 6. New Orleans (La.)—Fiction. 7. Science fiction.] I. Title.
PZ7.L43844Loo 2013
[Fic]—dc23 2012025510

Reinforced binding

Visit www.un-requiredreading.com

THIS LABEL APPLIES TO TEXT STOCK

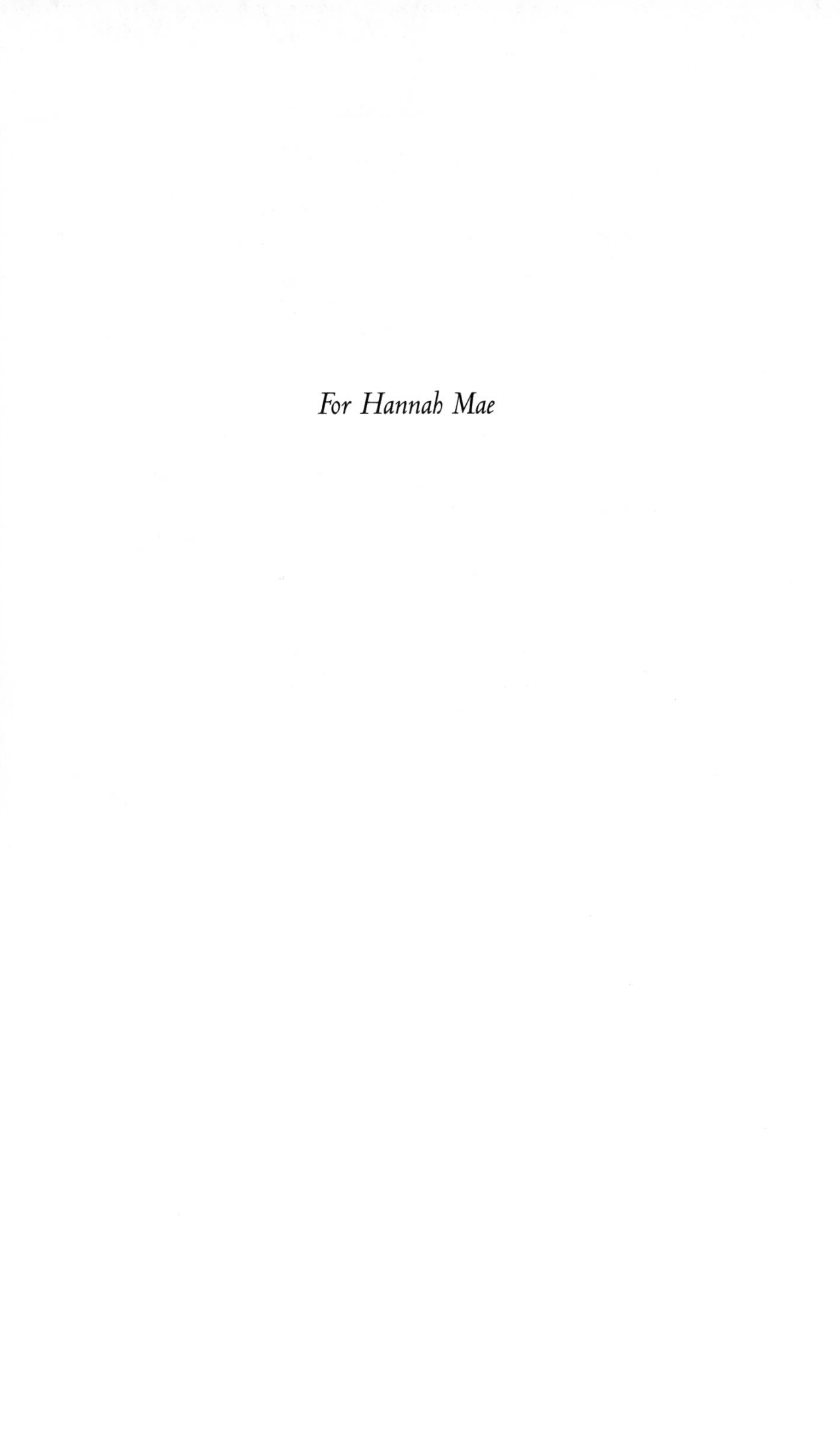

For Hannah Mae

one

"This is it, Ben." Maggie's eyes are wide, pupils big and black like puddles of ink. "This is when it happens." Her gaze bores into me. "We can hide, or we can fight."

I look around at the mountain of toilet paper, the stacks of cardboard boxes full of shampoo and cigarettes. "Fight? With what? Should we throw combs at him? You have plans for a tampon cannon or something?" I kick a rusty bolt across the floor. "We're screwed, Maggie."

Her face softens, dread fading into grief. She sighs and her whole body deflates. "Yeah, we are."

She's still clenching my arm, stopping the blood from flowing to my hand—but I don't say a word. Maybe I make her feel better just by being there, even if I'm only something to be squeezed.

"Maggie?"

"Mmm."

"I'm sixteen years old. I don't want to die in a Walgreens."

She smiles, sad and sweet. "It won't be the first time, Ben. And hey"—she lets go of my arm and takes my hand—"maybe this is the one. Maybe we get it right this time around."

"Maybe." But I don't believe it.

The squeal of a rusty hinge splits the silence of the stockroom, and Maggie's eyes widen, panic spreading from her face to mine. "Here we go," she says, her voice unsteady.

She stuffs the envelope into the waist of her jeans and drops to her knees. Reaching under a crate topped with cases of bottled water, she emerges with a two-by-four that has three rusty nails sticking out of one end. Though it's only a few feet long, it makes for one gruesome weapon.

Maggie hands it to me, then reaches under a nearby shelf, coming up with a long steel hook—the kind used by warehouse workers to drag heavy pallets around.

I turn to slip behind a low shelf, and Maggie grabs my arm. "Not there," she says. "You get shot in the face there."

I shudder and find us a spot behind cases of air freshener. Crouching low, I realize that my breathing is heavy, and I try to muffle it with my hand. Every little movement, every heartbeat sounds a hundred times louder now, and I'm afraid that all the noise will give us away.

I try to slow my breathing. I try to calm my heart, but it just beats that much faster.

And in walks Roy.

I hear him before I see him, his shoes echoing across the concrete floor. I feel cold all over, my skin turning clammy and my fingers trembling. He stops within spitting distance. His voice is deep, reverberant in the expansive stockroom. "You know it's over, you little bastards."

His shoe makes a soft *shhh* as it pivots on the cement; he turns toward us, homing in.

Before I can stop her, Maggie springs, swinging the hook at his chest. She misses by inches as Roy takes a neat step back, watching as Maggie falls to the floor. One quick jog forward, and his shoe is on her neck. He fakes a yawn, nodding in my direction. "Your turn, junior."

I rise slowly, legs weak, everything numb. He points to my board with its twisted nails. "Drop your little club, Benjamin."

I nod, but before letting the two-by-four slip from my hand, I twist my whole body, wind it up like a corkscrew, and swing with everything I have.

Roy barely has time to react as one of the nails tears through his cheek and draws blood.

Then, in one smooth movement, his right hand sweeps forward, and I see the gun. Small, black—almost anticlimactic. The muzzle flashes bright white, and the sound of the shot rebounds off every surface in the stockroom.

My chest is on fire. I land hard on the concrete, head turned toward Maggie. Her eyes are filled with terror as Roy lifts his shoe from her neck, bending to take the envelope of cash from her jeans.

She pulls in a deep breath and whispers, "I love you," a moment before he presses the muzzle to her temple and fires a second time.

That's the last thing I see. My right arm grows warm as my own blood pools around it—everything else feels cold. I suck in one last stuttering breath before it all turns to black.

And I die.

two

MY MOM PURSES HER LIPS, arms folded. "You swear you'll be back by dinnertime?"

"Cross my heart."

"You *promise?*"

"Yes, Mom, I *promise.*"

"If you spend your bus fare on junk, I'm not coming to get you."

"You're killing me, Mom."

She eyes the kitchen clock, then me, then the clock again. "Okay, fine. Go. Have a good time. And—"

I'm halfway out the door when she snatches me by the collar. "Don't eat anything. Dinner will be ready when you get home, and if you push it around your plate all night because you filled up on beignets or whatever it is you eat down there, we're gonna have some words."

"I know, Mom. I love you!" I yell over my shoulder as I hop down the steps to the street. I'll do my best to keep away from the beignets, but it's not easy. Mom is a pretty awesome cook, so that's some incentive right there. I think tonight she's roasting a chicken—which means Dad will be in charge of making the gravy, and that is *definitely* a good thing.

I get off the bus at North Rampart Street and walk through the French Quarter toward the river. I come here as often as I can, really—I love everything about the Quarter, except maybe the smell of Bourbon Street. The whole strip stinks of rotten beer. It collects in murky puddles, warmed by the sun until it evaporates into warm, reeking, beer steam.

But other than *that,* I love everything about the place. The *other* smells are amazing, the smells that spill out of restaurant kitchens—sautéing onions, garlic, and peppers.

But the best part is the music.

Music is everywhere in New Orleans. You can hear horn blowers and guitar players on almost every sidewalk, four-piece hard rockers blasting cover tunes from the bars on Bourbon, jazz combos playing to full rooms on Frenchmen Street. Most guys my age aren't really into jazz, but to me a trumpet in the right hands is as close to heaven as you can get.

Usually, when I get to the Quarter, I head straight for Jackson Square. For almost three centuries, this has been the social center of the French Quarter. It's a big open space by the river, where artists sell their paintings and fortune-tellers offer tarot and palm readings dirt cheap.

You get what you pay for, Mom always says. *Not that I'd pay for that nonsense, but if I did, I'd sure want more than five bucks' worth.*

However, today, as soon as I get off the bus, I immediately feel strange. I keep getting little flashes of déjà vu.

I've had déjà vu before—I'm pretty sure everyone has—but it usually only happens once in a while. Today, it's like every time I turn a corner I'm slapped with that feeling, the sense that I've experienced this exact moment before. I feel like I've seen the same couple of tourists—I recognize their matching LSU sweatshirts in particular—though I can't remember when or where. And just as the sensation starts to fade, I get the same feeling about a stray cat lurking behind a potted palm tree.

As I reach Jackson Square, the feeling gets stronger. And it's like I'm a little more *ahead* of it. Instead of just a feeling or an impression that I've been in this moment before, I feel like I'm in control of it. Like being aware you're having a dream, but without waking up.

I close my eyes but I still see the square in my mind—a sunny afternoon just like this one, though a few details are different. For one thing, the people milling around aren't the same. In my mind, there's a family of four, all in matching fleur-de-lis shirts, on a bench across from me, but when I open my eyes they're gone. And the music coming from the café down the block is a different song than the one I hear in my head. But the temperature, the light, it's all the same.

I move farther into the square, take a seat on the steps of the Saint Louis Cathedral, and close my eyes again. Immediately, I'm immersed in a vision, a waking dream. I know I can open my eyes at any time, but I'm too curious, and I let the vision unfold.

In my mind, I'm moving toward the far end of the square, approaching a small folding table under a big blue umbrella. In the shade of the umbrella is . . . Steve.

I know Steve—I haven't actually met him, but I *know* him.

I see him wave as I walk closer, motioning to the empty seat across from him at his little table.

A sign is propped against the side of the table. It reads TAROT READINGS BY PSYCHIC STEVE $5. But Steve doesn't look like a psychic. He seems about my dad's age, a little gray hair in places, kind eyes. He has a friendly face. Altogether, he looks like someone's Little League baseball coach.

He doesn't speak at first, just grins and begins laying tarot cards out, though he isn't paying attention to them. There are creases around his eyes from smiling at passersby and squinting into the sun. He stares out at the tourists and the palm trees, and sighs.

"Benjamin, I just love it here."

The vision disappears, as though the movie in my head has hit the end of the reel. I open my eyes and I'm still sitting on the cathedral steps. But now Jackson Square is exactly as it was in my mind—the band down the block is playing the same song I heard, the same family with their matching fleur-de-lis T-shirts are now sitting across from me.

It wasn't déjà vu. It was something else, something . . . *real.* Like peeking behind a curtain at some alternate reality. It was a moment I know I've felt before, yet it seems like something that is still to come.

I notice my palms have started sweating, and I wipe them on my jeans. My throat is dry, and it's hard to swallow.

Did I see the future? The past? Both?

Then I glance across the square, and I see the blue umbrella. Leaning against the table is a sign: TAROT READINGS BY PSYCHIC STEVE $5.

Steve waves and offers a grin.

three

STEVE SMILES WARMLY as I approach. He motions to the empty folding chair across the table, and I sit down.

"You're Steve, aren't you?" I give him a dubious look.

"Yes, I am." Now that I'm closer, I see something in his eyes that doesn't really sit right with the friendly uncle vibe I got at first. His eyes are gazing into mine, his mouth is smiling, but his mind is clearly not on board. I can't help thinking the next time he blinks, the green irises and black pupils will be gone, replaced by swirling red pools of fear, mischief, and anger. But then he chuckles, and suddenly he has a whole new face—one like the joker in a deck of cards, an unhinged grinning clown.

I scoot back a few inches in my seat. "I think I just saw this moment. Only a minute ago."

"You may very well have," he says with that creepy jester grin.

"So I saw the future?"

"No, Benjamin. You were just remembering. Remembering this moment."

The feeling of déjà vu isn't gone, but hovers in the background while I focus on making sense of what Steve is saying. It's disorienting. "But how could I remember something that hasn't happened yet? That's like . . . *pre*membering."

Steve scoops up his tarot cards and shuffles them slowly. "Ah, all will be explained, kiddo. You *are* remembering me. You just don't realize it."

When I open my mouth to speak, he blurts precisely what I was about to say, and we speak in unison: "So when did we meet, then?"

He chuckles and points his index finger downward, thumping the table. "Right here, just a moment ago."

"That doesn't make sense."

He laughs. "No, I suppose it wouldn't. But I don't want to confuse you any more than I need to." I expect him to continue, but instead he just stares at me in silence.

Steve grimaces and fishes around the inside of a bright red plastic Igloo. "In my cooler here, I have two bottles of Dr Pepper." He hands one to me. "Drink up."

"Thanks." I take the bottle eagerly.

Steve pushes his palms into his forehead as if trying to rub the wrinkles out. He slams both hands down on the table and barks, "Ha! Crash!" His voice turns whiny and meek as he mimics a child crying. *"Mama! Owie . . ."*

Behind him, a small boy on a bicycle, fresh off his training wheels, wobbles into an older woman taking a picture of the cathedral. Both hit the pavement. *Crash. "Mama! Owie . . ."*

I catch Steve's eye and am about to speak, but he stops me with a nod. "I know. Weird, right?"

I want to grab him by the collar and yell, *JUST TELL ME WHAT'S GOING ON RIGHT NOW!* But instead I simply shake my head and try to keep my cool.

Steve sweeps aside imaginary fog between us with a flourish of his wrists. "Okay, here we go. Picture, Benjamin, a stream."

"Easy enough." I marvel at my own willingness to follow his direction—this guy I just met a minute ago. At least I *think* I just met him a minute ago. Feels more like I've always known him, but—

"Now, think of the current in that stream as Time. As the water flows past, so do the days and weeks."

"Still pretty easy."

"Okay. Now picture a rock or a stump in that stream, and imagine the way the current swirls around it, circling back on itself, over and over. That's called an eddy."

I form a picture in my mind of a current whirling around a large rock, circulating and recirculating. I'm beginning to relax, but I'm doing this with my eyes open. Not sure I trust this nut enough to close my eyes with him sitting right there. "Got it. An eddy."

"Once in a great while, Benjamin, there's an obstruction in

the current of Time. I don't really know what causes it. I'm not sure anyone does. But sometimes, Time will circle back on itself just like that eddy in the river. It cycles and recycles, over and over and over. It's called a Time loop."

Clearly the man is insane. Still, a part of me is intrigued—and another part of me doesn't want to antagonize a head case unless I have a good running start.

"So Time ends up circling instead of flowing straight on?" I mean to say it with confidence, but it comes out sounding like a question.

"You're pretty sharp, for sixteen." Steve sips his soda. "Now, do you know what that means? How that affects those people caught in the loop?"

How much weirder is this going to get? "People get caught in the Time loop?"

"Of course." That smile again. Like he could just as easily be screaming, but *smiling* won the coin toss.

I shake my head, somehow unable to just walk away. It's too interesting, too . . . familiar? I'll humor the old guy another minute or two, but that's it. "Okay, so what happens to them, then? The people in the loop?"

"Well, for one thing, eventually they find each other. They gravitate to one another. Their lives begin to mesh."

"How does that happen? I mean, how do they find each other?"

"The way you found me today. You were sort of pulled here, weren't you?" Crazy grin.

A quiet settles between us, and Steve gives me time to think it over. I let my gaze wander over Jackson Square, suddenly even more uncomfortable when I remember that intense déjà vu I had before I came over to his umbrella.

I steady my voice and try to sound relaxed, but the soda in my hand trembles as I say, "You're telling me I'm in a loop."

"Of course you are. But you knew that, didn't you?"

I manage an awkward smile.

"The thing about Time working in a loop, Benjamin, is that nothing really changes from one cycle to the next. It's the same thing, over and over."

"Sounds boring."

Steve grits his teeth, but says, "Actually, it's not so bad. I've learned to focus and remember details throughout my trips through the cycles—and I use those memories to make my life very easy. I know who to put my money on in the World Series this year, and what day to buy my lottery ticket."

Steve can spin a pretty interesting story, I'll give him that. "So, like . . . how long is your loop? A year? Two?"

"Less than a month." He says it like he's remembering he has cancer.

"Mine too? A month?"

He waves his hand dramatically, like shooing away flies. "Nah, you're more like a couple of days, I think. And your loop is pretty new, so you don't have the crazies yet, like I do. Wait till you've been through it a few thousand times, then we'll see how the old brain is holding up." He pushes a finger into my forehead as though I didn't know where my brain was.

"So I've lived this day a whole bunch of times already, then?" Might as well play along, earn my Dr Pepper.

"Yup, you've got it."

"Is everyone in my life in a loop, too?"

"Nope. It's pretty unusual for somebody to share a loop with someone else. It does happen, though. Like you and Maggie. But most of these people"—he waves a hand across the square—"most of these people are leading normal, linear lives. We're a bit of a rarity," he says.

A bolt of electricity blasts through me, from my toes to the top of my head, and every hair stands on end. *Who's Maggie?* I manage to put together a few short words. "I'm not sure I understand." Understatement of the millennium.

"You will," Steve says. He smiles that friendly uncle smile, the one with the creepy eyes that are focused on some time or place normal people don't go.

"So why don't I remember any of it? This all seems pretty new to me."

"That's the thing—you don't really keep your memories from one cycle through the loop to the next. But little by little, it's possible to store a tiny sliver of an experience here, and a short memory there, each time you circle around in that stream. You probably recognize these little memories as déjà vu." Steve grimaces. "Me, I've been through mine so many times, I remember damn near everything. Every little stupid face that walks by, every . . ." He drifts away, his mind elsewhere.

I feel chilly, yet sweat beads up and rolls down my back. "So . . . we've had this conversation before?"

"*Many* times before."

"So, if it's so boring, why don't you just do something else? Move away, make new friends, try a—"

"Because you just *can't*," he snaps. "It's not some fun, live-forever thing. It's a trap, where you do the same thing every time. You can't just move off to Houston, or make a new friend, because that's not what happened last time. You can only do what you did last time." His face is red.

"Nothing changes at all?"

Steve massages his forehead again. "Little things. Inconsequential things. Over time they can add up, but big changes, no. Nothing changes. It's too hard."

I close my eyes and give it a minute to sink in. When I open them, Steve has risen from his chair. His frustrated face is suddenly a mask of serenity. Talk about mood swings.

He places a small sign that reads BACK IN FIVE MINUTES on his table. "So long, Benjamin. There's a guy who's going to propose to his girlfriend over by the French Market. It's beautiful, I never miss it." He turns from me and saunters off across the square, toward the river. I stay behind and wonder if I know what will happen next.

four

I STILL HAVE A COUPLE OF HOURS to burn before I have to be back home for dinner, so I take the ten-minute bus ride to wander through the mall, still gripped by the feeling I had in Jackson Square. I buy an iced tea in the food court and decide to wander the second level while I try to wrap my head around what Psychic Steve dumped on me back in the Quarter. The man was clearly a lunatic. Fascinating, but still a lunatic.

I pass a store that sells cooking stuff—cutlery, pots and pans, fancy salts that come from the Dead Sea or wherever. I love all that stuff. For a second I think about stopping and filling out a job application, which would get Dad off my back about *earning my keep* and give me something to do for the summer. I wouldn't mind a few bucks in my pocket, either. But I figure I'll come back later in the week, when I'm wearing something nicer than a T-shirt and jeans. Maybe I'll even comb my hair.

My mind is in another world as I drift through the crowds toward the escalator. No matter what idea I start with, it always finds its way back to Steve.

Psychic Steve.

Psycho Steve.

That whole scene bothers me for so many reasons that I can't even pick one to focus on: He knew my name. He had the eyes of someone from a Stephen King book, and not the wise old *advice-giver* kind, but the super-scary *lost his mind to the dark side and wants to chop you up* kind. And the way I felt like I'd stuck a fork in the toaster when he said the name Maggie . . .

I step onto the escalator and let it carry me upward as I gaze at the shoppers below. Lots of families today. The heat tends to drive folks inside—the movie theaters are probably pretty jammed today, too.

At the top of the escalator, she slams into me like a linebacker. My iced tea splashes down the front of my shirt and pants. The ice makes me gasp.

And Maggie grins.

I stand rooted to the spot, in the way of everyone stepping off the escalator. I get jostled and shoved, but I don't move or take my eyes off her face.

I *know* her, just as I knew Steve.

The moment I meet her gaze everything freezes, and while time is stopped I study all the details. Her long reddish-brown hair falls past her shoulders, one side tucked behind her ear and the other hanging in front of her face. Her eyes are dark brown, so dark they almost look black; and tan freckles dot each cheek. The one ear I can see is pierced a gazillion times.

She's absolutely beautiful.

She has a backpack slung over her shoulder, and her mouth is fixed in a smirk as she watches the tea run down my chest.

"Last time, I actually knocked you over," she says.

She doesn't speak again, just takes my hand and leads me, darting through the crowd until we reach Macy's. We weave through racks of clothing, past the jewelry counters, beyond the fitting rooms, and skid to a stop in front of a door with a panic bar and a red and white sign that shouts EMERGENCY EXIT. ALARM WILL SOUND. Maggie puts her hand on the bar.

"But—the alarm," I say.

"The alarm won't go off," she says. She pushes the door open and we're off again, down a set of cement stairs outside a loading dock.

The alarm doesn't go off.

The bright day explodes around us. Everything is white-hot and blinding, and I shield my eyes from the sun, pulling in a long, deep breath.

"So you're Maggie," I manage to say.

She nods with approval. "Nice one, Romeo. You didn't remember my name last time. Come on, we have to move. I want to get ahead of him this time, save us a ton of trouble."

"Get ahead of who?" I need time to make sense of *whatever* is going on. She doesn't give me any time. Instead, she pulls me by my shirt, and I stagger along behind her. We run along the side of the building, sticking to the shaded walkways and ducking under tractor-trailers. Maggie seems to have a pretty good idea of where we're headed, but she doesn't take the time to let me in on it. I'm just doing my best to keep up.

As we run, she looks over her shoulder, not at me but beyond, as though keeping watch for someone who might be following. That gets me looking over my shoulder, too. I don't know what I'm looking for, but I sure don't like how concerned Maggie is about it.

We barrel around a corner, headed toward Seventeenth Street, and crash into a man in a yellow T-shirt and jeans. All three of us end up on the ground. I'm slow to get up, checking myself for scrapes and bruises, but Maggie is already on her feet, scrambling for something that flew from the man's fist when we collided. The man in the yellow T-shirt scrambles for it, too.

Everything is coming so fast, and I can't register all that's happening. It's just a blur. All I can seem to make sense of is that I need to stay with Maggie. I need to keep up with her, do what she does.

Maggie and the man in yellow claw at the pavement, clambering to reach the thing that has skidded across the sidewalk in the collision.

It's a gun. And for some reason I know it's a semiautomatic, and that it sort of smells like burning matches after it's fired.

The gun clatters on the cement walkway and slides to

a spot near Maggie's fallen backpack, just out of the man's reach. His eyes widen when he spots it, and widen further when he sees Maggie pouncing on it.

The eyes: I know them. The face, the clothes, everything. I know them all.

The man in the yellow shirt and jeans might as well be Death himself. My whole body reacts to his presence. Muscles clench, my heart beats double-time, adrenaline races through my system.

I pull myself free of my natural inclination to lie on the concrete frozen in fear, and I yell the name that's in my head, the name stored in the same little vault that held Steve's name.

"Roy!"

five

MY SHOUT MAKES THE MAN PAUSE, ever so slightly, his gaze straying from the gun for just a split second, then flashing toward me in pure surprise. Recognition shoots across his face before he turns his attention back to the gun. But he's too slow—I buy Maggie the moment she needs to beat him to it and snatch the gun away.

Roy kneels, hands slowly raised, his face a study of concentration. He forces a creepy grin. "Well . . . this is new, sweetheart."

Roy is a big guy. Muscular, but not in the polished gym-rat way—he looks like a guy who used to be a boxer but let himself go. His face looks like it may have taken a few shots too, with its crooked nose and one eyebrow with a white scar running through it. There's something generally *asymmetrical* about his face, like maybe one cheekbone sits a little lower than the other. He has a fighter's posture, too, that hunched-over stance like he'd been in the middle of a bob-and-weave drill and just got stuck that way.

Maggie shakes her hair out of her face. "Shut up." She jerks the gun toward the man, and he flinches ever so slightly, drawing a sly smile from Maggie. She levels the gun at his chest. "I could kill you right now. And I'm thinking that I should. Shouldn't I, Benjamin?"

She knows my name!

It makes sense, of course—I know hers, and somehow I know Roy's—but hearing her say it sends a shiver through me.

"Shouldn't I, *Benjamin*?" She speaks forcefully this time.

"Uh, yeah—I mean, whatever you think is best."

I can't believe that's what I come up with. *Whatever you think is best*? Come on. If this were a movie I'd get killed just for delivering such a lame line. And things have gotten weird enough that I'm not sure this *isn't* a movie.

Roy smiles, tentatively at first, and then becomes more confident, and stands. He brushes the dust off his sleeves. "You won't kill me. That's not how it goes. You can't change the big picture, Maggie." He takes a step toward her. "You can mess around with the details now and then, sure. Like Ben's little ad-lib there. But you can't change the master plan."

Maggie inhales, hands beginning to shake from the weight of the gun, or maybe just from the weight of the situation. She tenses every muscle; her jaw clenches in determination as she grips the gun and squeezes the trigger.

The blast from the muzzle surprises us all, and the sudden bite of gun smoke hits my nose, slapping me out of my daze. The expression of disbelief on Roy's face makes me feel sick—it isn't the way they make it look in the movies. He doesn't jerk backward and drop like a bad guy in a James Bond film. Instead, he puts his hands to his ribs and sinks to his knees, his eyes wide and full of fear.

Maggie stands frozen, the gun still smoking, her hand still trembling. For a moment, she wears Roy's same look of disbelief, as though she's the one who's been shot.

She snaps out of the shock and snatches her backpack from the ground. "Come on, we have to get out of here."

six

Maggie has me by the hand again, pulling me along the side of the building, back the way we came, toward the mall. The sound of the shot has already drawn people outside to check out the action, and it occurs to me suddenly that we weren't the only ones on that street.

Somebody must have seen Maggie shoot Roy.

I look over my shoulder and catch a glimpse of Roy crawling toward an idling car. The driver stands outside his open door, leaning down to offer help, and I think I see Roy reach up and grab the man by the wrist before we turn a corner. We race up the steps of a loading dock and into the shadows.

Maggie opens a steel door, passing a man in coveralls as we run through. He puts up a hand. "Sorry, missy," he says. "Ain't a mall entrance. Back the way you come."

"A man's been shot," Maggie gasps. "Out that way." She points over her shoulder, and without a second glance, Mr. Coveralls scampers outside. Maggie yanks my arm, ready to run again, but I manage to hold her still.

"We're going back in the mall?" I ask. "Shouldn't we be running *away*? Like, to anywhere but *here*?"

"We're safe this way," she says. "Don't worry."

Sure. Why worry? We've only managed to shoot a guy on the sidewalk. With witnesses. My stomach does a flip as images of prison jumpsuits and electric chairs flash through my head.

How did I get here? Not here on a loading dock outside the mall, but *here*—hand in hand with a girl I met two minutes ago, barely enough time to introduce ourselves, yet clearly enough time to bond over attempted murder. From a high-school nobody to felon in 120 seconds. My thoughts lock up like rusty brakes when I try to process what has just happened.

Maggie grabs me by the arm, and once again, we're off.

More dashing through the mall, past window displays with headless mannequins and girls in aprons offering free samples of warm pretzels and cubes of cheese. We slow down when we hit the thickest part of the crowd, and Maggie lets go of my arm. We pause for a moment to take a breath, and I scan the faces around me for a sign that news has spread about a shooting outside. So far, it looks like the word hasn't gotten out. *Yet.*

I hide my shaking hands in my pockets. "I really would

feel better about a hundred miles from here," I say. "Or in Mexico. Yeah. I'd feel *much* better in Mexico."

Maggie nods, her gaze fixed farther down the mall, past the food court. "Mexico would be nice, Ben. But right now we're not going to get anywhere looking like this." She gives me one quick scan, head to toe. "No, this is no good."

"What? What's wrong with how I look?" I take stock of my look in the window of a shoe store. Sure—jeans, an iced tea–stained shirt, and a mask of terror won't get me into the best club in town, but considering the circumstances, I think I look all right.

Maggie smirks. "You look fine, Romeo. We just need to not be so . . . identifiable."

I resist the urge to deliver an awkward compliment, something like how she shouldn't change anything about herself, how she looks awesome just the way she is, and . . .

Maggie nods in approval. "This is where you're supposed to say that stupid line about me not changing a thing. Good for you—you're getting better at this. We might have a chance yet."

Wait. This is where I'm supposed to say what?

She turns and grins over her shoulder. "Makeover time."

I follow her to JCPenney, the crowd already thinning at the news of random violence outside. Bits of conversation come our way, fragments like, *police everywhere out there,* and *a gang of kids shot someone in the food court.* There's a noticeable increase in the number of police officers milling around, too.

We head for the salon at the back of the store. A woman

is sweeping up trimmings, building a mountain of hair on the floor, while Maggie and I pause just out of sight by a display of styling products. At this point I figure Maggie knows what she is doing, so I don't bother to ask. I'm just trying to keep up and not get us in more trouble than we are already.

Maggie leans in close and whispers, "Scissors, over by the combs and brushes there. See?" She nods to our right. "When the phone rings, the lady with the broom is going to turn her back and walk toward the front desk. You're going to grab the scissors and meet me in the ladies' room, over there by the water fountain."

I say okay, but my brain is starting to buckle under the weight of all the questions I have. Scissors? Am I even *allowed* in the ladies' room? Is this even *real*?

Before I can ask, the phone at the desk rings. As Maggie predicted, the woman with the broom straightens up and turns away from us. Maggie gives me a hard shove, and I make for the scissors.

I run like they do in war movies—crouched low, head down, using shelves of shampoo and hair products for cover. I scurry to the scissors and snatch them up, pausing for just a second to look at the price. *Twelve bucks?* I'm not impressed and I grab a cheaper pair, fully aware that I am not just shoplifting but still managing to look for a bargain. Mom would be so proud.

I breathe a long sigh of relief as I find the ladies' room unlocked and empty. Just as the door eases closed behind me, it swings open and Maggie slips in, pushing the lock in behind her with her elbow. Her hands are full.

She piles her stash on the sink: an empty plastic spray bottle, a comb, hair clips, and a towel. I look at my lonely scissors and add them to the pile.

Maggie pulls the scissors out of their packaging and looks me over. "You first. Sit."

Like a mute puppy, I obey, turning a plastic wastebasket over and taking a seat while she runs a comb through my hair, assessing the situation and finally taking a fistful of it in her hand.

Snnnnnip.

A lock of blond hair falls to the floor, hair that had taken me so long to get just right. Then more falls, and more, and soon the floor around me is covered in it. My head feels noticeably lighter. I watch Maggie in the mirror, focused and serious, and try not to think about all the ways my life has changed in the last fifteen minutes. Or how many times I may have sat here before, thinking the same thing. Or about why she's so much better at remembering what comes next than I am.

"Maggie?"

"Yup." She doesn't look up from her work, the *snip* of the scissors an inch from my ear.

"This is really happening, isn't it?"

"Yup."

"This is a loop. Like Steve was talking about."

"Who?"

I don't know how I'd explain Steve, and honestly I don't

have the energy to try, so I let it go. Maybe I'm dreaming—seems a lot more likely that I'm making this up in my sleep than actually sitting in a women's restroom getting a haircut by a stranger in the mall after being an accessory to murder.

But what if it's not a dream? Sure doesn't feel like one.

"Roy said that this was new, Maggie . . . you shooting him. How come you knew what to do then? How did you know the lady would turn her back when the phone rang, and all that?"

She grins. "Roy doesn't always have the best memory for this stuff. He can retain a lot, I mean a scary amount, but he doesn't seem to remember that we did it this way last time. And as long as he doesn't start remembering better, we'll have the edge on him. We'll know what's coming, and he won't."

"So he's not dead."

"Nope. Just winged him."

"And he's still going to come after us," I say. I somehow *know* that—like the way you just know not to eat cigarettes. A combination of logic and instinct.

"Unfortunately, the loop has a way of setting things back on track. A little gunfire is just a bump in the road, Benjamin. He'll be back, and he'll be pissed."

Maggie crouches in front of me, eye level, her gaze switching from my right ear to my left. "It looks even enough."

I swallow hard. "Is it even *enough*, or is it *even*?" Like that's what's important right now.

Maggie grimaces. "Even enough."

Not the diagnosis I was looking for. I stand, brush the clippings off of me, and check myself out in the mirror. Actually, it isn't too uneven, but it *is* shockingly short. A whole year of growth, lost.

Next, Maggie stands over the sink and starts on her own hair, cutting it far above her shoulders. She works fast and smooth, and as the hair falls away and more of her face is revealed in the mirror, I can't *not* look. Her dark eyes, the way her lips naturally turn up at the edges so that she always has this little smile going . . . Trust me, you'd stare, too.

Of course, when she's done cutting, she looks perfect. I position myself behind her and compare our new haircuts in the mirror. I definitely got screwed.

Maggie pulls a box of black hair dye out of her backpack. The dye stinks. Five minutes later, her head is an inky wet mess. She sits against the wall. "Twenty minutes, Benjamin. We have twenty minutes to kill."

"What happens in twenty minutes?"

"I wash the dye out and we get the hell out of here."

"What do we do until then?"

"Last time, I sat here and answered all your questions."

"Oh." I sit against the opposite wall and try to focus, but my mind is totally jumbled. "Do you remember every little detail of what's coming? Like what my next question will be?"

"No, not every detail. Hopefully I remember most of the important ones, though. But in general I'm pretty good at remembering things from one cycle to the next, and holding on to a few memories of the cycle before that, and even a little from the one before that. You, Benjamin—you're not so good at remembering."

"But *why*? It's not fair. You have this awesome power, it's like ESP—and I have nothing. I get to follow you around and try not to get us killed."

"I know it feels unfair. And it's not a power, it's experience. But we all have our talents, and yours is something . . . else. We'll figure it out, Ben. I promise."

I stuff my hands in my pockets and stare at my shoelaces. I'm probably pouting, too—I'm not usually aware that I do that until Mom calls me on it. But I feel like the last kid picked for a team on the playground. Like I'm a liability.

"I'm trying," I say.

"I know you are. And already you're better at remembering things this time around than the last." She lowers her gaze. "Still, I wish I had your memory."

"You mean you wish you sucked at remembering all this?"

She smiles. "I'm bored, Benjamin. And frustrated, and pissed off, and scared. This isn't my first loop, you know—I've been caught in them before. This is my fifth. But the first four didn't go on as long. This one just seems . . . eternal. So it's like there's never anything new, and it feels like there never will be. I can't change the way it's going to go . . . or at least I can't seem to do it on purpose." She shakes her head. "It sucks."

A terrible realization comes over me, starting as a little knot of nausea in my gut and spreading over my whole body as I put the words together: "This loop is different because we die in it, don't we?"

Another little gem that I somehow just *know*.

Maggie barely moves her head, but it's still a nod.

"Do you remember dying, Maggie?"

"I do remember, yes," she says quietly.

"What's it like, then? To die?"

"It's like . . . well, it's always a surprise, no matter how prepared for it you are. And I've become pretty prepared for it. It's like it never actually seems possible that I failed, that Roy was faster, or smarter, or stronger—it never seems possible that it's over, that I couldn't beat him."

She leans closer to me. "And I feel stupid. I actually feel embarrassed that I'm dying, that after I'm gone I'll leave this ugly body there for someone to deal with. I'll just be a corpse on the floor that will traumatize the first person to find me. And my last statement to the world will be 'I lost.' I'll just be another dead body, and nobody will ever know, never understand, what it's like to go through it over and over."

I bump her with my shoulder. "Except me."

She smiles at that. "Except you."

seven

THE MALL IS BUZZING when we slip out of the restroom. The police are everywhere with radios, notepads, and dogs, searching the stores, combing the crowds, taking witness statements and stopping anyone who looks under thirty.

That doesn't bode well for us. Not at all.

Maggie doesn't seem too concerned, though. She leads me casually through the mob, shadowing a tall couple for a while, then ducking into a store for a moment just as an officer with a noisy radio strolls past. Once, we stand and wait while two officers finish their coffee just around the corner, only a few feet away. But Maggie knows they won't look our way, so she motions for me to be still and waits calmly despite the two cops being so close we can hear their conversation.

"Load of crap, if you ask me," says one.

"How's that?" says the other.

"Come on. We're supposed to find two teenagers in the mall on a Saturday afternoon? There's gotta be a few hundred of 'em in here. And they all pretty much look the same, am I right?"

"Ain't wrong."

"Damn straight. Neil expects us to grab every kid we see with a stupid haircut and jeans on? Gimme a break."

"You tell 'em, Ron."

The cops stroll off toward the food court, and we shadow them, Maggie knowing that they won't bother to look over their shoulders, and before long we peel off and slip through an exit, back in the sunlight and walking nonchalantly south on Causeway Boulevard.

"Give me your phone," Maggie says.

I fish my cell out of my front pocket and hand it over, watching as she tosses it into the street. It makes a sickening crunch as it disappears under the tires of a passing car, reappearing as a mosaic of shards of black plastic and gray buttons, and I feel like I've been kicked in the gut.

"Hey, what the hell?"

Maggie doesn't answer, just pulls out her own phone and repeats the process. *Crunch.*

"Our phones are traceable, whether we're actually using them or not. By the end of the day the cops will have enough witnesses' descriptions of us that you and I will be identified as the two kids who shot that poor old guy at the mall. Our phones would lead them right to us. Sorry about that, Ben."

I stare at the electronic carnage on the asphalt and try not to show my heartbreak. "That's okay," I say.

We walk in silence for a few minutes before I think to ask where we are going.

Maggie runs her fingers through her still-wet hair. "Toward Downtown. We're going to spend the night at a place I know while we figure out the next step."

"You mean a *different* next step. I'm assuming that you know what it is we usually do, and we're looking for something that'll turn out better, right?"

She laughs. "You've got it. But, yes. We always head for Shreveport in the morning, and that's kind of a major step toward us getting killed, so we're going to see what we can do about pushing ourselves in a new direction."

I find myself wondering if we die in Shreveport, if that's the last stop for us before we start the whole thing over again and I meet Steve in Jackson Square. I want to ask, but I don't want to know the answer, so I keep my mouth shut.

I must be focusing on it a little too much, because Maggie bumps me with her elbow and says, "Breathe, Benjamin. We don't need you freaking out just yet."

I let out a long breath I hadn't even realized I'd been holding. "Does that mean I can freak out later on, then?"

Maggie laughs. "Yes. There will be a time to freak out. But not yet, so chill."

We get on the bus a few blocks away from the mall, and I'm grateful to find a couple dollars in my pocket. I have a hard enough time acting cool; I don't need to ask Maggie to spot me bus fare.

The bus rolls down Causeway Boulevard, stopping every few blocks to let a few passengers out the back and let a few new ones in up front. At one stop, a police car rolls slowly past, and Maggie and I duck down low in our seats, even though we know the officer probably can't see inside.

"You know," I say, "if we just hand ourselves over to the cops, Roy won't be able to get to us. Not as long as we're locked up."

Maggie nods. "True. He probably wouldn't be able to get to us, but that's because we'd be locked up for a long time. A long, *long* time, Ben."

"Not necessarily. I'm sure we'd get cleared if we got a decent lawyer. Right?"

"Seriously? Benjamin, I shot a guy that, as far as everyone else is concerned, I'd never even seen before. And I don't think anyone saw him holding the gun on us. No one even looked in our direction until after I fired, and then they just saw me holding a smoking gun and Roy laid out and bleeding. Not a good picture for a prosecutor to paint, Ben. And don't forget, you're an accomplice."

"So on one hand, we have a very good chance of going to prison, and on the other, we have a very *slim* chance of not getting killed in Shreveport and living a normal life afterward."

"That's pretty much it, yeah."

I slouch in my seat. "I'm not too excited about either option."

"Me neither, Ben, but at least you and I get another shot at getting it right one of these times. Dying sucks, but we'll be back right here before you know it, giving it another try. But prison . . . nah. That's just sitting around, waiting to die for good."

She's right, of course. I get the feeling that she's right a lot.

Maggie turns toward the window. "That's where my house is. Six blocks down that way, one block toward the lake."

I nod. We're too far from my neighborhood in Gentilly to bother pointing out the direction.

It occurs to me that I will probably never see my home again. I may never see *New Orleans* again. My mom, dad, my school, friends . . . In any other situation, the thought of never going back to school would have me giddy with joy, but sitting here, on the bus, it's just depressing. And scary.

At the end of the line, we take another bus toward Downtown, getting off at Saint Charles. Just as I'm opening my mouth to ask how much farther we're headed, Maggie says, "A few blocks north. You can see it from here. Look."

She points straight ahead, and three blocks away, a large tan building looms. It looks like a warehouse. "That's the Mission," she says.

"What's the Mission?"

"It's our room for the night. Don't worry, I have friends there."

eight

THE MISSION TURNS OUT TO BE a homeless shelter, the biggest I've ever seen. According to the old woman at the door, it's actually the largest in New Orleans.

The building looks like an airplane hangar from the outside, and a little bit from the inside, too. Steel girders span the ceiling, and round ductwork snakes through and under, all painted matte black. Huge flat lights like electric trash can lids hang from cables in the ceiling. Some of them buzz.

Maggie leads me to an office. An older black man in a white shirt and blue tie looks up from his computer. His smile is warm and welcoming. "Maggie. I'm so happy to see you." He rises and nods his head. "And you brought a friend."

Maggie puts her hand on my shoulder, only briefly, but long enough for me to miss it when she takes it away. "Pastor

Joe, this is my friend Benjamin. Benjamin, Joe."

We shake hands. "You look like a fine boy to me, Benjamin. I am pleased to meet you. You here to volunteer?"

I look to Maggie for the answer. "Actually, Joe, I wanted to show Benjamin a little about what you all do here. You know, take him around and maybe talk him into putting in some time. Is that all right?"

Pastor Joe laughs. "Well, of course it's fine with me. Show him whatever you want. We need all the help we can get."

"Joe, do you suppose maybe we could spend the night, too? My mom has a million friends over, you know—book club or something. They'll be drinking wine and laughing loud until dawn. I mean, if you have the beds free."

"Oh, we have a whole mess of open beds for you two. The weather's so warm, nobody wants to sleep inside much. Can't blame 'em. Gets hot as hellfire in here during the day, and it doesn't cool off until morning, almost." He shakes his head. "That's some tour, though. Your momma okay with you spending the night?"

"Of course," Maggie says. "Do you want to call her?"

"Goodness no, you're all grown up anyway. Not my place to tell you what to do. You've been good to us for a long time, Maggie. You ever need a bed or anything else, you know you're welcome to it."

Maggie beams. "Thank you, Joe."

I can't imagine the place ever running out of beds. There are bunks, three high, filling a room that looks big as a football field. We take bunks in a far corner, two top ones side by side.

"I've been volunteering here for a couple of years," Maggie says. "Turns out to be a great place to crash or hide out. It came in handy last time." She fluffs her pillow. "And here we are again."

My stomach is growling. "Do you think—"

"That there's any food around? You got it. Follow me."

Maggie puts her backpack on a hook in the hallway and leads me through the big bunk room to the kitchen at the rear of the building, where there are shelves stacked high with bread, sacks of potatoes, and huge cans of broth. One shelf is nothing but giant cans of coffee.

"Feel like a sandwich?" She grabs some bread and a jar of peanut butter from under a counter and begins putting together a few sandwiches. "Not much variety here usually, but once in a while we'll get a donation of something interesting. A big load of fresh veggies, you know—stuff like that. It's not always good, though. Pastor Joe told me about one time, maybe a year after Katrina, they were so low on food that they had to hand out MREs that the army left here."

"MREs?"

"Stands for 'Meals Ready to Eat.' It's what soldiers eat in the field. They last forever, literally. We still get donated crates of them every once in a while. A few of the meals are all right, but most are just gross." She laughs. "We'll grab a few before we go, just in case."

I shudder, praying it won't come to that. I doubt that prepackaged military meals are preferable to going hungry.

We eat our sandwiches in silence. When we're finished,

Maggie starts laying bread out on the counter, two rows of twelve slices. "We're making extra sandwiches for the kitchen to hand out later on. I usually make a couple dozen."

I turn to Maggie. "About the mall."

"I was waiting for you to ask."

"I have a lot of questions," I say.

"I know. I'm ready. Fire away."

I take a deep breath. "Roy."

"You really want to know?"

"No, not really."

Maggie smiles sadly and hands me a knife and a jar of grape jelly. "Benjamin, however many cycles, however many trips through this loop it's been since it began, Roy has killed us. Every single time."

I give this a minute to swirl around in my head as I decide whether to believe her or not. I mean, I've seen some weird things in the past few hours, but really—should I trust an insane fortune-teller; a girl I've never even seen before; and a few bouts of déjà vu?

Apparently I already *did,* and now I'm hiding out in a homeless shelter hoping the cops don't drag me to prison for attempted murder. Might as well hear her out. "Go on."

"It started when you and I met in Shreveport. We won some big money at the horse track." She points at the jar in front of me. "Start spreading, slacker."

I run my knife over the bread. "Shreveport? Never been, never wanted to go. That makes absolutely no sense whatsoever. Oh, but—" I pause.

"What?"

"I'm remembering that last week my friend's dad was talking about going up there for some kind of work thing soon. Maybe I was going to tag along?" Great, now *I'm* crazy, too.

Maggie continued. "I don't remember it too clearly, but I think I talked you into helping me cash in a big winner at the track. We needed an adult to collect our winnings, and we gave him a cut or something like that. Anyway, Roy was hanging around outside and figured out that we won big—we weren't very good at hiding it, I guess. He followed us, stole our money, and killed us in the process."

"How?"

"Keep up, my part's done already." I look down at my five finished slices. "He had a gun. He shot you, then me. The first shot may have been an accident; I don't remember it, exactly. I kind of remember him panicking."

This is insane. Ridiculous. Yet my stomach tightens the way it used to when I was little and had to get the needle at the doctor's office. That pure, sickening *dread,* knowing what was coming. It seems my body already believes what my brain isn't ready to.

"And that's been happening ever since? Each trip through the loop? We die in Shreveport?"

"Bingo."

"Wait," I say. "If the loop started when we met each other up in Shreveport, how come you and I met in the mall this afternoon? I thought it was supposed to go the same way every time."

Maggie nods. "I know. The thing is, it doesn't always go *exactly* the same way, from one time around to the next. There are always a few little things that might change—details—but over the course of however many trips through our loop, those little changes can add up to a big shift. Like human evolution. We didn't just one day climb out of the oceans as *people*. We started as slimy little flipper-creatures, in the beginning. It took millions and millions of years, and lots of little changes, but here we are, making sandwiches in New Orleans."

I start putting sandwiches together while Maggie lays out more bread. My fingers shake. "Sounds kind of hopeless," I say, trying to sound casual.

"Right?"

"But at least we have you."

"What about me?"

"Maggie, if you remember everything from one cycle to the next, that's like . . . *serious* power. You can see what's coming, and—"

"I can see it, but I'm not so great at changing it."

I resist the urge to suggest otherwise; instead, I clamp my mouth shut and swallow the words.

"Hey, you did it again," Maggie says. "I think you were supposed to say 'Sure you are,' but you didn't."

I shrug. "Maybe that's my talent. Changing things."

"Maybe."

"So we make a pretty good team, then?" Despite the sinking feeling in my gut, I can't help smiling. Having Maggie next to me makes me feel that maybe all is not as hopeless as it seems.

"I suppose we do, Benjamin."

We look up at the same time, and our eyes meet. Maggie taps the back of my hand with the peanut butter knife, and laughs. I look for a rag to wipe off the peanut butter, but not before smearing her wrist with jelly from my knife. I can't help laughing, too, even as my pulse races.

Maggie leans past me to grab a paper towel off the counter just as I turn to find a rag, and we almost collide, our noses an inch apart. Our faces are so close that all I can see are her eyes; her dark, laughing eyes. I realize instantly that there is nothing I want more right at this moment than to kiss her.

Whoa! Easy, tiger. You've known her for two hours. Moving a little fast, aren't you?

I can feel her breath on my cheek.

You can't kiss a girl you met two hours ago. Seriously.

It kills me to do it, but I lower my eyes and back away, wiping the peanut butter off my hand. Maggie grins proudly, as though she just won a game of chicken. Which she may have.

"Okay, Romeo. Next question."

Sigh. Back to business.

"So what comes next? Like, how is it supposed to go in the end so I know what to watch out for? I have no idea how to change things, but I know we won't have a chance if I don't know what needs changing."

"That one's a little tougher. It's not always exactly the same."

"Yeah, but how did it go last time? That's how it works, isn't it? Whatever happened the last time is what will happen again if we don't change something."

"Yeah, you're right, but I may not be remembering exactly what happened the last time. I could be remembering the time before that, or the time before that. So, I can't guarantee that I'm right, but from here . . . I'm pretty sure we stuck with the usual plan and went for the money."

"The money?"

"I know which horses will finish first, second, and third tomorrow night at Louisiana Downs. All I need is an off-track betting joint and an adult willing to take a cut for placing the bet, and we'll have a sackful of cash."

I can't begin to imagine what that kind of bet would rake in. But "a sackful" sounds about right.

"Over the course of our trips through the loop, our plan has turned into using the winnings from the track to get the hell out of Louisiana. Disappear and get Roy behind us forever."

I'm beginning to put it all together. "But once we get the money in our hands—"

"Roy is there. He's always there. All he has to remember is to be at the OTB tomorrow night. He's dumb, Benjamin, but he can always remember at least that much of it."

Maggie's voice is calm, but her eyes are beginning to show the hopelessness beneath. "I just wish there was someone we could trust enough to ask for help," she says. "Someone who wouldn't think we were crazy."

"Steve," I say.

"Steve? I don't think we've met; I'd remember it. Who is he?"

I choose my words carefully. "He's . . . he's a little on the crazy side. Well, more like a *lot* on the crazy side, but he tried to explain the loop to me. I didn't really believe him at the time."

"I don't blame you. When was this?"

I pause as a sudden, ominous rumbling rolls through my stomach. "This morning in Jackson Square. He mentioned your name—you may not know *him*, but he seems to know who *you* are."

Maggie thinks this over, biting one of her nails. "Is he in a loop?"

I nod, feeling queasy but trying not to show it. "I guess it's a pretty serious one. He remembers pretty much every little thing that's happened. Or will happen. Or . . . whatever. You know what I'm saying."

"Can we trust him?"

That's a good question. "I don't think it would hurt to talk to him."

"Okay, then," Maggie says, but doesn't seem convinced.

"What I'm saying is that I think he can help us. Or at least he'll listen and not think we're insane, like everyone else would. Maybe he'll have an idea or two about staying out of Roy's way."

Maggie rests her chin on her hand, elbow on the counter, her new black hair hanging across half of her face. She looks me straight in the eye, and I fight the instinct to look away. I'm unsuccessful, and our eyes lock for what feels like an hour. She dabs my nose with a dot of peanut butter and smiles sweetly. I blush, despite the suspicion I may have eaten something I shouldn't have. At least a little blushing puts some color back in my face. I'm pretty sure I look pale right now.

"So then tomorrow we'll try to see Steve," she says.

"Try?"

"We're supposed to go to Shreveport in the morning, so get ready: It'll take all of our will to fight it and get ourselves into the French Quarter instead."

"How much time do you think we have? I mean, when does it . . . you know. *Happen?*"

Maggie deflates a little. I can tell too much talk about our fate is taking its toll on her optimism. "Like I said, things tend to change a little here and there from one cycle to the next. Details, mostly. But one thing that has *never* changed is the time it happens."

I wait for her to continue, my palms sweating.

"Sunday night, nine thirty."

Right now it's four o'clock, Saturday afternoon. We'll die in twenty-nine hours and thirty minutes.

nine

MY STOMACH FEELS BETTER pretty soon after our talk about going into the Quarter, the queasiness passing uneventfully. Thank God.

We spend the rest of the evening hanging around the Mission—warm as it is inside, it's way too hot to go out and wander just for the sake of wandering. We have no money to spend on food or entertainment anyway, so we resign ourselves to playing blackjack in Joe's office and talking about anything but dying.

At blackjack, she beats me every hand. I mean, *every* hand. So I'm wondering if it's because she remembers which cards will come up, or if it's because I suck at blackjack. And *that* gets me thinking about the conversation we had about going into the French Quarter to meet Steve instead of getting on the bus to Shreveport—did we have that talk the last time through the loop, and Maggie just doesn't remember it? How would we even know?

It was weird that my stomach was doing flips the whole time we talked about breaking out of the loop. . . . Maybe that's what it feels like to do something new.

Neither of us sleeps much. I can hear Maggie turning over all night, trying to get comfortable on her cot, and I do the same. I want to say her name and talk some more since we're both awake, but I don't think that's supposed to happen, because I can't seem to will myself to speak. So I lie there until the sun comes up, my stomach in knots over what's ahead.

We have a quick breakfast with Pastor Joe: cold cereal, wheat toast, and grits. *Really* bad coffee. But I'm starving and glad to have it.

Following the plan, we stop by the kitchen on our way out, and Maggie puts a couple of MREs in her backpack. The boxes are labeled CHICKEN ENCHILADA WITH SAUCE, but I can't imagine an actual meal fitting in those thin little boxes. And they certainly don't weigh enough to convince me that I won't still be starving afterward.

I begin to think, What I wouldn't give to be able to swing by home and pack up some of Mom's roasted chicken . . . and I realize, Mom and Dad may not have eaten dinner at all. At first they were probably annoyed that I was late and holding up dinner, but then as minutes and hours passed, their annoyance would have turned to worry. Their worry would have turned to fear, and they would have called the police at some point. The police would have told them I was a suspect in a shooting at the mall.

They wouldn't believe the police, me being a good kid and everything. But part of them would wonder.

Maggie's parents probably went through the same thing.

Maggie slept on her hair funny, and seems grumpy after a restless night in a strange bed, but she still looks amazing. It really doesn't matter what her hair is doing as long as I get to see her eyes now and then. I try to say so, but I chicken out before I can even get to the first word.

We say good-bye to Pastor Joe and thank him for the sandwiches and beds, then head out into the morning sun. The bus stop is one block away, and we walk there in silence.

And so begins one of the strangest battles I had ever waged: the fight to *not* get on a bus.

"I'm counting on you," Maggie says.

"Me?"

"Yes, you. Once we start toward the Quarter, I'll have nothing to offer. We'll be on a whole new cycle, nothing we've ever done before. There won't be anything for me to remember to help us out. And the only thing to keep us from slipping back into one of the old patterns in the loop is your willpower, Benjamin. It's up to you to get us to Jackson Square to see Steve."

"How hard can it be, though? We'll just make sure we don't get on the wrong bus. Right?"

"Ben, pretty much everything up to this point has been exactly the way the loop is supposed to go. To deviate from the loop is to resist the rules of the universe, to defy the power of Fate, or destiny, or whatever you want to call it. It's trying to prevent something that's *already happened,* which, by definition, is impossible."

Great. No pressure.

We wait some more. Finally, a bus comes into view. But Maggie touches my shoulder. "We don't want this one."

"Where does it go?"

"That's the one we usually get on to take us to the bus station for the ride to Shreveport. We want the bus after that. . . . *That* one will take us to Canal Street."

We watch the wrong bus approach slowly, creeping up the street block by block, stopping to let a passenger off before pulling away from the curb and lurching back into traffic.

My palms are sweating. I suddenly feel a tremendous urge to pull bus fare from my pocket and step toward the curb as the bus gets closer. The lack of control is terrifying, and not just because I'm not in charge of my own body, but because the force that wants to wrestle me onto the bus is virtually irresistible—and it has plans for me to die very soon.

"Mags?" I put my arm around her shoulder. "We should turn around and face the building. Now."

I start, turning one foot to the left and then the other. It's a monumental effort. Maggie's feet are less cooperative. I gently steer her away from the curb, pushing with my shoulder, until we face the building.

Her body is rigid with tension. "Ben, this feels *so* wrong."

She's right. My stomach is queasy and I'm breaking out in a cold sweat. She is, too. "I know. We'll get through it, though. Maybe . . . maybe the key is to anchor your body right where it is and just block out the bus. Mentally. Visualize the way you want it to go, too . . . Picture the bus leaving without us. Then focus your mind on something else. Anything else."

"Like what?"

"I don't know. Name the states."

"The *United* States?"

"No, the *Monkey* States. Come on—" I pull her closer to me. "Let's start on the West Coast."

She closes her eyes, and I can't help staring at her face—the way her eyes squeeze shut tight and her brow wrinkles as she begins naming states. As she carefully enunciates each syllable, I focus on her lips. They look soft. I imagine kissing them, and for an instant I've forgotten about the insane situation we're in.

That is, until she says, "Washington. Oregon. California."

The bus is one block away, pulling closer to the sidewalk to make our stop. I try to keep my focus on Maggie and the states, but I suddenly have this sick feeling, like my insides are trying to escape. Every molecule in my body is rejecting the fact that I'm not digging bus fare out and getting ready to board the bus. My body knows what I'm trying to do, and it doesn't like it. Not at all.

"Arizona. Um . . ."

I try to collect myself and whisper, *"Nevada."*

"Nevada. Idaho. Utah. Ben, I don't feel so good."

"Me neither. Keep going."

The bus pulls up behind us. We must look ridiculous, standing with our backs to the street at the bus stop, and even more ridiculous when the bus waits and we don't get on.

Maggie's hands are balled into fists, sweat beading up on her neck. "Montana. Idaho."

I swallow hard and try not to vomit, noticing now that there's *pain*—from the center of my body, from the middle of my bones, everything hurts. "You already said Idaho."

"Don't be an ass. Wyoming. Colorado." Maggie makes a gagging noise. She's pale, and I know I must be, too.

The driver gives up on us and closes the doors. The bus creeps away.

Maggie opens her eyes. "New Mexico." She turns her head and watches the bus roll south, her skin shiny, almost white. "Texas."

I still have my arm around her. "We're all done with the states, Maggie." I want to act cool, but my whole body is shaking.

Maggie exhales a long breath. She looks exhausted and worn down, as though she just ran ten blocks. "That was a lot harder than I thought it would be."

She steps to the side, and my arm falls away. The sickness is fading, but the feeling that my body is trying to reject *everything* remains. This entire reality, everything, from the sidewalk under our feet to the air in our lungs, it's all wrong—we're not supposed to be here. Not here, and especially not *now*. We've messed with the order of where things should be in space and time, and every cell we have wants us to be on that bus to set it right.

But as the seconds pass, the feeling subsides little by little until the shaking in our hands settles a bit and our cold sweat turns back into normal, gross, Louisiana afternoon sweat. I'm still queasy and weak, and I can tell Maggie is, too, but at least I'm not in danger of vomiting myself inside out.

She gives me a quick glance, and though it's brief, in it I can see I've earned some respect. I've impressed her.

She catches a bead of sweat that is heading for the tip of my nose with her thumb.

I smile.

We wait, side by side, as the bus we want creeps into view.

ten

GETTING ON THE BUS to Canal Street is a lot easier than *not* getting on the one before that. Maggie notices this, too.

"I guess we're in uncharted territory, in a way," she says. "It's like the loop hasn't really figured out what's supposed to happen yet. I feel . . . free?"

"Me too. Like a dog off the leash."

She grins. "Yeah. Exactly."

From Canal Street, we decide to walk, even though the heat has me practically hallucinating. We slip through the Quarter, following Royal Street, keeping to the shady side of the road. Now and then we duck into a store to soak up the air-conditioning or dodge the gaze of a police officer.

Maggie says, "I was thinking that if we figure this out and not get ourselves murdered in the next day or so, I might try to find a job. We should both find jobs, Ben." A bead of sweat trickles down her neck, and despite the heat, I find myself following its path along her throat, my pulse quickening as it disappears down the front of her T-shirt.

"For the air-conditioning?"

"Yup, you got it."

It's not a bad idea. By the time June rolls around, pretty much any excuse to find air-conditioning is good enough. "What kind of job do you want to get?" I ask.

"Oh, I don't know. Something easy. No restaurants. I don't want to work late or smell like food. And nothing in an office."

"Why not an office?"

"Mom says cubicles destroy your soul."

I smile at that. "My dad says pretty much the same thing."

"My dad lives in Baton Rouge," Maggie says. "It's just me and Mom at home."

"My parents are still together. Dad works a lot, but Mom is always home." I choke at this last thought. Will I ever see them again?

"I'm betting you have a lot of friends," Maggie says.

"A couple good ones. Jeremy Brenner and Lucas Pierre. A few others I'm nice to but don't actually like that much. You?"

"None."

"None?"

"Well, this kid Mike Carter is nice to me. I guess I could call him a friend. He only has nine fingers."

"How'd he end up with only nine?"

"Long story. I'll tell you all about it sometime. But other than him, no. No friends."

"That's not possible."

"Oh, yes it is." She smiles sadly. "Remember I said this wasn't my first loop? I've been in four others before this one. I was pretty young for most of them. But the more times I went through the cycles, the more stuff I'd pick up and remember the next time through, so pretty soon I was acing tests I didn't study for and predicting which kid was going to get sick on field trips. I knew what everyone was going to say before they said it. Got me a reputation as a witch."

I nod, not sure what to say.

"So what kind of job would *you* want to get?" she asks.

I laugh. "A restaurant. I don't mind working late or smelling like food."

"For real?"

"Yeah. I love to be in the kitchen. I love knives and flames and garlic in the pan. I make better fried chicken than my mom, and she's the best cook anywhere."

"Is that what you want to be? A chef?"

I nod, though the idea of growing up to be *anything* now seems unlikely, at best.

We cross into Jackson Square, with the Saint Louis Cathedral towering over us. Around the edge of the grassy lawn, artists have hung their paintings on the wrought-iron fence, and a man spray-painted gold, head to toe, stands on a crate and poses like a football trophy. A boy no older than thirteen tap-dances on the cobblestones, bottle caps riveted to the soles of his shoes. The kid must be on the verge of heatstroke. If I had a dollar I'd put it in the coffee can by his feet.

At the end of the square, Steve sits at his table, gazing off toward the river. His arms are folded, and he looks ready to nod off to sleep.

I stand quietly behind Steve as Maggie takes the seat across from him, slipping off her backpack and letting it slide to the ground. I wait to see if there will be some recognition between the two.

He gives Maggie a cordial nod and begins laying tarot cards in front of her, though he barely glances at them as he places them down. He checks his watch and grins.

"Check this out. Watch that guy on the unicycle."

Across the square, a short man dressed as a clown is juggling bowling pins atop a unicycle. Suddenly, he lets the pins fall and swings off the seat, throwing his leg into the scrambling feet of a purse-snatcher. Man and purse spill onto the sidewalk.

Steve smiles. "There's a cop right on the other side of the fence there. He'll be along in a second."

Steve watches the purse-snatcher rising from the pavement on wobbly legs, and Maggie takes the moment to study his face. He's wearing the same put-on mask of serenity, a thin curtain of a smile that doesn't quite cover the storm clouds underneath. He lowers his eyes and mutters to himself, and it only takes a second to realize he's mimicking the conversation that's going on behind him between a mother and her daughter.

I nod to Maggie. "That," I say, "is Steve."

At the sound of my voice, Steve spins in his seat and gasps. "Benjamin!"

I plop down in the empty seat next to Maggie. "Hey."

His eyes widen as his mouth hangs open. "Benjamin," he says again, shaking his head in slow motion.

"Steve, this is Maggie. Maggie, meet Steve."

Maggie offers her hand. Steve's shock melts into a knowing smile as he takes it, pumping up and down excitedly. The shake goes on longer than one should, and Maggie has to put some muscle into pulling her hand away. Steve just keeps nodding and grinning. "You've done something big, Benjamin. You've done something really big. This is brand-new."

"It wasn't easy."

"I'm sure it wasn't. All those trips through the loop, you and I, and I've never seen you twice in the same cycle. Never. And now—" He holds his head as though it's going to explode. "Here you are. And nice haircut, by the way." He mimes *haircut* with his hand, snipping the air.

I run my fingers through my new hair, still marveling at how weird it feels. "Thanks. Maggie cut it."

Steve shakes his head, beaming excitedly. "Oh, Benjamin . . . you've done something *big*."

Now he has me a little worried. "Steve . . . *how* big?"

"Well, it's hard to say for sure. From my perspective, this is the biggest change I've seen in your loop. There's no telling what can happen from here. But I suspect Maggie would know best. Maggie?"

"This is all new to me."

"Is it? Well, congratulations, then: You've learned how to bend Fate. Too cool."

"Bend Fate?"

"Yup, bend Fate. You can't push Fate in another direction completely, but you can nudge it and send it just far enough off course to disrupt the loop. And if you disrupt the loop, you just might be able to slip out and rejoin the stream to float on." Steve extends both arms, making little waves with his hands.

"We did all that just by not getting on a bus?" I ask.

Steve draws a long breath. "Well, it's hard to describe, kiddo, but yeah—that's exactly what you did. First, you became aware of it, right? You felt your loop pulling you in some direction or another, didn't you?"

Maggie and I answer in unison: "Definitely."

"Okay, so you try to tune into that feeling. You need to be aware of the loop's pull so that when another event occurs that seems familiar—something you remember from a previous cycle—you can try to change it a little. Give it a push and see if you can revise the outcome." He winks like he just showed us a really great card trick.

Maggie shrinks in her chair. "But just getting on the right bus nearly wiped me out. I don't know if I have it in me to change Fate on a regular basis."

"You're not changing it entirely. You're just putting a little bend in it. One small shift in your actions can lead to bigger changes further on." Steve leans in close, motioning for us to move closer as well, and whispers, "I have confidence in you two, I really do." He says it like he's afraid of being overheard.

I give it some thought, but it's hard to share his optimism. Now that I know what it takes, I can't imagine the strength we would need to turn our lives in a new direction altogether.

"I don't know, Steve," I say. "Maybe it's hopeless. If we're meant to die, maybe we're just meant to die."

He cocks his head to one side. "Not as long as you keep fighting it, kid. Every time you bend your way out of a scrape, the loop is going to try to find a way to sweep you back in. I can promise you that. So don't let your guard down, not for a second." Steve grits his teeth and puts an iron hand on my shoulder. "You have more power in you than you realize, though, Ben."

I give Maggie a wistful glance. "I hope you're right."

Steve laughs excitedly. "Come on! You're on a whole new cycle, you two. You have no idea how sad it is when I see Benjamin come walking across the square and sit down at my table, time after time after time." The happy Steve face vanishes in an instant, replaced by the somber, serious Steve face: "Every time I see him, I know it's happened again and I know he's going to wind up the same way in the end." He draws a finger across his throat and lets his tongue drop out of the side of his mouth. "But now . . . now *anything* can happen."

Maggie pulls her chair closer. "Steve, do you think we've changed enough to escape the loop? Have we—"

"Stirred it up enough to slip out?" He shrugs. "I guess it's possible. Hard to tell right away. Generally, you need to do something pretty big. Huge changes. Really shake it up, you know?" He spreads his arms out all the way to show us *just* how huge a change we need. "Of course, loop or not, you'd still have a problem."

Maggie grimaces. "I guess you know about Roy?"

"Yeah. I see the story about him in the paper the next day, you know—after he kills you two. I read it every time. The guy's a first-rate psycho on a mission. He doesn't care about your loop; he's busy with his own. He just wants to do his job, what the loop tells him he's supposed to do. But—" Steve draws us in again, beckoning us closer until our noses almost touch. "That's not all of it. I'm thinking he's got it in for you guys."

Maggie rolls her eyes and shrugs. "Duh. He's murdered us over and over. I'd say, yeah, he's probably got it in for us."

"No, I mean, I'm betting he's *afraid* of you. The thing about getting stuck in a loop, a really bad loop like mine, see, is that it messes with your head—"

Maggie says under her breath, "Clearly."

Steve doesn't seem to hear. "The thing is, it makes you paranoid. You just want out, right? But the repetition, the boredom just turns your brain to oatmeal, and pretty soon you're not thinking right. And I'm thinking at this point, Roy figures you'll be trying to kill him to break out of your own loop. To him, see, it's like a 'them or me' situation."

Maggie and I exchange glances. My guess is that Steve is either way off base or totally on the money. I just have no idea which.

We watch a police officer drag the fallen purse-snatcher to his feet, the cop nodding gratefully to the clown, already back on his unicycle with juggling pins in the air.

I turn to Maggie. "What's next, then? Where do we go from here?"

Maggie shakes her head. "I don't know. But it feels like . . . we could do *anything*. Right?"

"You feel it, too?"

"Yeah. I didn't realize how many little decisions the loop made for me until I was out of it."

She's right. It's completely foreign. It's probably what freedom feels like.

"Hard to tell what's next, really," Steve says. "I suppose you two should keep focusing on not slipping back into the old cycle. What would normally be happening for you at this point?"

"Right now we're supposed to be on a bus to Shreveport."

Steve sits back and rubs his chin. "Then the next move seems obvious to me. If the loop says go north, well, you two should head south."

"Good idea, but we're in New Orleans, Steve," Maggie says. "There *is* nothing south."

"Yeah, I suppose you're right. Well, east, then. Slidell. Gulfport, Biloxi, whatever. Just, you know . . ." He nods gravely at Maggie. "Just stay the hell out of Shreveport between now and tomorrow."

"I guess we can manage that," Maggie says. Then she turns to me and leans in close. "Right, Ben?"

Across the square, I see the police officer is looking in our direction, his gaze fixed on our little table. His hand goes to his radio and he speaks into it, his eyes still on me.

I turn to Maggie. "That cop over there. Looks pretty interested in us."

"Maybe our makeovers haven't fooled him."

The cop cocks his ear to the radio, his eyes narrowing as he listens. He starts in our direction with his ear still to the radio, nodding as he walks. He lowers one hand until it rests on the grip of his pistol.

I grab Maggie by the arm. "I think it's time to go."

eleven

Now I have Maggie by the hand, pulling her through the tourists as we tear down Chartres Street, sprinting across intersections and winding our way around taxis lined up at the curb on Decatur Street. Maggie might have led the way at the mall, but the French Quarter is *my* hangout, and nobody knows it better than I do.

We head straight for the river, and though I have no plan in mind, I *do* know that if we are going to outrun the cop, we aren't going to do it dodging all these people wandering the streets. We shoot across Decatur and straight through the outdoor seating of Café Du Monde, darting between tables of tourists eating beignets and drinking café au lait.

Maggie leaves a remarkable trail of devastation in our

wake, pushing over every chair or table that we pass, forcing the cop behind us to leap over them, or better yet, get tangled in one or two and hit the ground.

Of course, this approach does nothing to keep our profile low. Pretty soon we attract enough attention to draw two more officers to us.

We speed behind a line of shops, the brick walkway at our feet a rusty blur. I hold Maggie's hand in a white-knuckle grip as we cut through a gap in the shops, then back onto Decatur Street, my brain finally cobbling together a plan to lose our pursuers in the crowd. And when you need a crowd, there's no better place in the city on a sunny morning than the endless rows of trinket-filled stalls of the outdoor French Market.

We rip through the last block of stores on Decatur and into the French Market, swerving between tourists and their shopping bags of tacky gifts and cheap sunglasses. Stalls whip by, beads and alligator heads on our left, knockoff handbags on our right. Maggie accidentally slams into a table and sends pewter figurines of fairies everywhere.

The cops are still on us, close enough that we can hear their footsteps as loud as our own. One of them yells out to us, but the words don't register. I just focus on the next move.

I lead us back across Decatur and straight through the front door of Coop's Place, one of the Quarter's older restaurants. They aren't yet serving lunch, but luckily for us the front door is ajar while a girl mops the entry. Maggie yanks the door closed behind us, and instantly we hear one of the cops slam into it, followed by the click of the latch as he tries to force it open. The door is set to lock when closed. A rare bit of luck going our way.

Through the dining room, past the bar, into the kitchen. The smell of garlic, boiling shrimp, and hot oil is overwhelming, and somehow, despite running for my life from the police, I realize that I'm hungry. There is one person in the back, a huge tattooed man chopping onions. He stares as we rush past, headed for the daylight of the open door.

We spill out into a brick alleyway that leads to a cement courtyard lined with Dumpsters, bolting toward a wooden gate to our right. I pound the latch with my fist and leave the gate hanging open behind us as we jog down the quiet shade of Ursulines Avenue, then take a left onto Royal Street, where we slip casually into the herd of wandering art gallery visitors, catching our breath and giving our legs a much-needed break.

Maggie plops down on the front step of a gallery, her head tilted back as she gasps for air. "What's our next move, Ben?"

I'm bent over with my hands on my knees, pulling in as much air as my lungs will hold. "Catch a bus," I gasp. "Get back to the bus station so we can hop a ride east. Gotta hurry, too—we need to get there before the rest of the beat cops get our descriptions."

"Probably a little late for that," Maggie says. "I bet we're all over their radios by now."

We make our way to the bus stop on North Rampart, walking quickly but casually. We glance behind us at every corner, but luck is on our side and we seem to have lost our chasers. It strikes me as a little odd that we could lose the cops after running only a few blocks, but it's good news, and I don't have the energy to question it.

Maggie stops me and points down at the sidewalk. "Hey, look at that," she says. "Bus fare."

Two twenties and three one-dollar bills lay face up on the concrete, pinned under the leg of a bench. I scoop them up.

Nothing wrong with found money, I think.

I steal a glance at Maggie, and she's eyeing the bills suspiciously. But sometimes good luck is just good luck and nothing more—right?

"What do you think, Ben?"

It's a silly question. We both know we threw off the cops a little too easily—the Quarter is not a big neighborhood. And now forty-three dollars happens to land at the feet of two broke kids who happen to need just that much to get out of town.

"I think we need to get out of the Quarter," I say.

She points at the money in my hand. "This doesn't feel like a trap to you?"

"Sure it does. But if the alternative is staying here and getting tossed in jail for attempted murder . . ."

Maggie grimaces, clearly weighing the situation as she glances from the money to the end of the block, where our bus would appear. "So we're walking into a trap set by the loop itself." She throws me a worried look as I hand her one of the twenties, and adds, "What's the worst that could happen?"

twelve

As soon as a bus rolls up, we pay our fare with the found money and sit down in the first open seats we see, completely on autopilot.

We switch buses at Canal Street. Autopilot. Step off at the bus terminal. Autopilot. Sit on a bench and wait in silence.

Maggie pats the bench. "Spent my share of time on this baby."

"Yeah?"

"This is where I catch the bus to Baton Rouge when I go visit Dad." She jabs a thumb over her shoulder. "I get off the city bus over there, pick up my ticket at that window . . . Dad is supposed to prepay, so I just give the ticket agent my name most of the time. Sometimes he forgets, though, so I always make sure I have cash before I leave the house. Then I come over here, sit, and wait."

"I bet you're usually not on the run from the police and counting down the hours to your death, though."

"No, not usually." It's pretty grim humor, but it seems to break the tension, and Maggie punches my arm playfully.

We go silent again and I can tell her thoughts, like mine, have turned back to the present.

Since leaving the Quarter, it's all been so easy. Too easy, maybe—seems like the loop even gave us the bus fare. I can't help thinking that it feels wrong, and my gut wants me out of that depot and headed elsewhere. Anywhere.

And now we're back to the same situation we were in earlier: sitting in the station trying not to get on the wrong bus. According to the schedule, there's a northbound bus to Shreveport and an eastbound one for Biloxi leaving within minutes of each other. Not much room for error.

At that moment, Maggie says what I've been thinking: "Ben, we need to make some changes. I think the loop gave us the money to get on the bus and be here together. Maybe the loop even sent the cops after us to force us onto the bus, so we'd think it was our choice all along." She looks around the station as though hoping for a neon sign to show her the right way to go. "Yeah, we need to make some *serious* changes."

She's right. We need to remove as many elements of Fate's plan as possible. We're already working on staying out of Shreveport, but that may not be enough.

Maggie puts a hand on mine. "We might need to split up," she says.

The thought stops my heart for a moment. But my heart also knows splitting up is our best shot at survival. It knew even before we got here, but I ignored it.

"No, seriously. Look . . . I think we might be making a mistake by being here."

I don't know what to say, so I just sit there like an idiot.

"I mean, if we've died together every time we've been through the loop, then . . . well, there's really only one way to make sure that doesn't happen again, right?"

I don't answer, just stare at the floor. I wonder if this really *is* all new, or if this is just a repeat of the last loop and Maggie doesn't remember as much as she thinks she does. I mean, how would she even know, right? Has she said these lines to me before?

"If we're always together when Roy comes for us in Shreveport, then the best way to keep us from being killed together is to just not *be* together, right?" She stares me down. "Right, Benjamin?"

I nod slowly. "I guess."

Maggie looks at the clock high on the wall. Our bus will be leaving in fifteen minutes. "So we should split up, then."

When she puts it like that, it has a shocking, dismal ring to it. For only the second time since we met the day before, she looks sad.

I shake my head. "There has to be another way. Right? I

mean, we're *stronger* together. If we split up we'll just both be weak."

She looks me in the eye, unblinking. "You know I'm right, Ben."

Of course I know it. But I don't *like* it. My heart pounds at the thought of us separating. "Okay, fine. But I'll take the Shreveport bus, and after I'm gone you get on the three o'clock to Biloxi. That's it—take it or leave it."

"No way. How come you're the one going to Shreveport? You know that's where Roy will be." Maggie's face is turning red.

I shrug. "Better me than you. And I'm betting that if one of us is there, maybe the loop won't worry so much about the other. A little distraction might do the trick."

Maggie shakes her head. "I don't like it."

"Look, if we both take random buses in opposite directions just to split up, the loop will still want us in Shreveport, and we won't be together, which means we'll be weak. But if one of us, you know—*volunteers* to go, that might be enough to let the other one slip out unnoticed."

"Quite a gesture, Romeo. But you don't remember all the details that you'll need to stay out of Roy's way. I do."

"But I'm better at bending Fate. I'll know what it wants me to do, and I'll push back. I can change it, Mags. All you'll have to do is get on the bus and stay on until you hit Biloxi." I put my hand over hers. "Please."

She looks at the clock again, though I can tell she doesn't

see it. She's thinking my plan over, looking for the cracks and flaws.

Apparently, she doesn't find any.

"You know that if one of us is going to get killed tomorrow, it'll be you, right?"

I nod. "Yeah. But I won't. I'll be fine. As long as you get on that bus, Maggie, we'll both be fine."

Silence. Probably three minutes' worth, the two of us sitting on the bench staring at the big clock.

Finally, Maggie sighs. "You know that after you leave, there's still another Shreveport bus that comes before mine leaves for Biloxi. I'll have a hell of a time staying off it."

"I know. I have a plan for that." I unbuckle my belt.

She puts a defensive hand out. "Whoa. Not so fast, cowboy."

"Oh, no . . . it's not what you think. I'm going to tie your hands together through one of the slats in the bench here." I feel my face getting hot. "You'll figure your way out, but not before the bus has left." I smile. "I hope."

"I was just giving you a hard time, Ben. I don't think you're a rapist." Maggie looks at the belt, then at the bench. "Well, if you come back in a few weeks and I'm still here, I want to be buried in Audubon Park."

"Maggie, if you're still here in a few weeks, it means we've beaten Fate."

"Right. But I won't care, Einstein. I'll be a corpse strapped to a bus station bench."

When my bus is ready to pull away, I leave Maggie with her hands held firm to the bench. She forces a smile as I climb the steps and weakly wave good-bye.

From my window seat, Maggie looks small. Her shoulders are slumped and her head hangs low. She looks up through her fallen hair as the engine rumbles and hisses. The bus pulls away from the station, and she grows smaller and smaller until we turn a corner and I can't see her at all.

I feel like I've abandoned her. No—I *have* abandoned her. But at least one of us will survive. If we stay far enough apart, Roy can't possibly find us both.

For a moment, panic creeps into me, tightening around my chest. Less than twenty-four hours ago I didn't even know there was such a thing as a Time loop—I was just going to the Quarter to hang out. Now I'm on a bus taking me to the place where my death has already happened countless times. I had confidence in myself when I first got on the bus, but now . . .

Then a calm settles over me as I picture Maggie. I imagine her growing up. Turning seventeen, then eighteen, going to college, getting married, and buying a house in a cute neighborhood on Lake Pontchartrain. Having children and grandchildren. Being *old*.

I can do this. I don't know *how*, but I know I *can*. I won't let the loop push me around. Or at the very least, I won't let it kill Maggie, too.

It's funny—I don't even know her last name. Or what her favorite food is, or what it was like growing up in her family.

But there's this *connection*—I know that's a cheap cliché of a word to use, but it fits—this *connection* that somehow lets me into the deeper stuff. I don't need to know her favorite color or when her birthday is, because I somehow already know that she doesn't worry about one color—she wants her life filled with lots of different ones. And her birthday isn't as important to her as her family's, because she's a giving person and she'd rather see someone she loves get excited over gifts than open her own.

So maybe I don't remember what happens in this loop. I don't know what's around the next corner or where exactly we're supposed to die. But a part of me remembers Maggie, somewhere deep inside, where all that prehistoric stuff is hidden—the instinct to run when you hear a swarm of bees, or the gut feeling that tells you not to put your hand in the fire—somewhere in that place where constants and absolute knowledge is kept, I know her. I know that we've been together so many times through this little loop that it's added up to years; and the thought of her taking a bullet and dying far from home is too much for me to give any thought to.

I sure as hell don't *want* to die. But I guess more than my own survival, I want her to live. And the absurdity of cashing in my life for hers doesn't seem so bizarre. It seems *right.*

Which is just crazy, because I only met her yesterday.

Gazing through the window at the blur of the passing guardrail, I silently answer the question that I realize my life had boiled down to:

Yes. I *would* die for her.

thirteen

I DECIDE TO GIVE BENDING FATE A SHOT. I've been on the bus for almost four hours, and I'm starving—my stomach is in knots trying to devour itself. The loop is pulling me to Shreveport, but it will have to wait; I need french fries.

The next stop is in a town called Alexandria, and as the bus settles to a stop and the doors open, I prepare to peel myself out of my seat and will one foot in front of the other until I'm down the steps and on the curb at the Alexandria bus station.

But even before we rolled to a stop, I got that sick feeling again. Judging by how easy it had been to get on the bus, how my feet had virtually walked themselves up the steps, I was already pretty sure I'd gotten sucked back into the loop. But now that I'm trying to get out of my seat and hop off early,

I know for sure. The trembling hands, the sweats, the feeling of my stomach squirming like a ball of snakes. My *bones* ache.

I manage to push the sickness aside and get to my feet, my body suddenly feeling like I'm packing an extra couple hundred pounds. My legs have turned to rubber and my knees shake under my own weight when I step into the aisle, placing one foot in front of the other as I make my way to the front of the bus.

Outside, there isn't much to see. The main drag runs straight through town, with a barbershop, a couple of convenience stores, an antiques shop, and a real estate office. Anytown, USA.

What I *don't* see right away is a place to eat. But it's not like I have any money anyway, and I'll definitely need a few minutes for my stomach to settle.

The street looks pretty much the same in both directions, but I choose to go right and stay in the shade. The sun has almost set, but it's still too warm not to keep to the cool side of the road.

I pass a store with a window full of electronics: cameras, laptops, portable Blu-ray players, iPods. Cell phones.

Oh shit.

Mom and Dad have to be *freaking* out.

I go in, fingers crossed for a phone I can use, but the best I can find is a laptop set up on the counter where you can Experience for Yourself the Lightning Speed of Our Fastest Network Ever. E-mail will have to do.

It's a small store, and the one sales guy is busy with a

woman looking at digital cameras. I log into my e-mail account and type as fast as I can.

> Hi Mom . . . I know ur probably afraid something really bad has happened to me or maybe the police have been to the house and told u i did something terrible but im ok, i promise. Hard to expln right now but im safe and everythings ok. Pls dont worry and ill be home soon as i can. I love u and tell dad i love him 2. Ben

I hit SEND and the message goes out with a *swoosh* sound, as though the laptop is actually firing my message, rolled up in a tube, off into space.

When the e-mail to Mom has closed, I see my in-box is still filling up. Mostly messages from Mom and Dad, and my friends Jeremy and Lucas. A couple are spam.

I can't believe I forgot to get in touch with Mom for this long. I just typed the first thing that came to mind, a few words of reassurance that will undoubtedly be analyzed by the cops and will end up being anything but reassuring. But what could I have written instead? *Hi Mom, all's well here. Met a girl, she's great, but shot a guy so we have to lie low until we get murdered tonight. Tell Dad I said hi too.*

Well, at least she knows I'm alive.

I clear the cache on the laptop and head back outside, staying to the shady side of the road.

Five minutes later, I smell bacon and follow my nose to a diner. Neon signs in the window promise hot coffee and breakfast twenty-four hours a day.

I take an empty booth in the back and open a menu. I'm flat broke but decide on a burger, fries, and a chocolate shake. I hate to order and bail without paying, but I'm being dragged by a time loop to a city where a man is going to try to kill me, and I can't fight for my life on an empty stomach. Sorry, Mr. Manager.

When my food comes, it takes me all of four minutes to devour almost everything. I run out of gas about three-quarters of the way through, and a handful of fries lie scattered on the scratched ivory-colored plate next to a little pond of ketchup.

As I'm scanning the diner for the whereabouts of the server and manager (such knowledge is the key to a successful Dine and Dash), the television over the counter catches my eye. Since I arrived it's been showing an ancient *Simpsons* episode, but now the local news is on and they're doing a story on a string of street robberies. The sound is turned all the way down, but the captions at the bottom of the screen give me the basics:

MAN SOUGHT IN THREE COUNTIES

ELEVEN ROBBERIES SINCE MARCH

All the while, an elderly woman is being interviewed on her doorstep by a female reporter who can't be a day over twenty-two, holding the microphone while the old woman appears to recount her own harrowing story of being mugged. She gestures wildly, first clasping her hands to her chest, then making a gun of her fingers and pointing it at the reporter, and clutching the sides of her head in panic. Hands back to her chest as the video cuts to surveillance footage of the suspect taken from a camera at a bank across the street.

It's Roy.

Even in the grainy monochrome video, I know it's him. His face is just a smudge of pixels in various shades of gray, but from the silhouette of his profile and the way he moves, there's no question. I feel goose bumps break out from the top of my head, spreading down all the way to my feet.

I'm glued to the screen, and while I would kill to be able to hear the audio, I don't want to miss a second of what I'm seeing to ask a waitress to turn up the sound.

The blurred shot of Roy cuts away to the reporter, microphone in hand, a look of grave concern plastered on her face that I'm not convinced is entirely genuine—I get the feeling she'd rather be covering a bigger story than the old lady getting her purse stolen. I can't read her lips at all, except for her very last words: *Now, back to the studio.*

It was just a little story on the news, maybe fifteen seconds of lousy video and no sound, but I feel like I've been shown a secret, given a chance to look backstage at the Roy Show. He's not just a monster who exists only in the moment he murders me, he's a *person.* An actual living person with a past and presumably, a future. More of a future than I have, anyway.

So Roy's a criminal. Not just tonight in Shreveport, but a criminal the rest of the time, too. Eleven robberies in two and a half months—is that a lot for a guy like that? I have no idea. Are there more that didn't get reported? Probably.

It makes sense, though, given what Maggie said about how he kills us over money. At least, that's how it all started. But now he kills us because he's in a loop and he can't do anything else. I know how that goes.

I let the video from the news play again in my head, hoping for a sign of weakness that I can use to my advantage. It starts with the old woman standing by the street. There's a sign for a bus stop next to her, so I'm assuming she's waiting for the bus. Roy enters the frame on the left, walking casually until he is right behind the woman—that's when he wraps his arm around her neck and waves the little gun in front of her face. She drops her purse, and he shoves her aside as he bends to pick it up. He jogs out of the frame to the right.

They had showed it three times through, then one more time in slow motion, and I had found no obvious weaknesses to exploit. He's in good shape, he's a big guy, and he clearly can't be swayed by pathetic old ladies. So I can rule out beating him in a fight or appealing to his conscience.

And then I wonder if he wishes he could change it. Does it bother him that he kills two kids over and over? If he has a conscience at all it would probably drive him insane. But now I remember the look on his face when Maggie had the gun on him back at the mall, and it seemed to be a game to him, a game he was so intently focused on winning that nothing else mattered, nothing else had meaning.

All these robberies—is he practicing?

I've been here for at least three hours, the remains of my fries room temperature and the weight of the loop oddly keeping me in my seat. I would have thought that Fate wanted me on the road to Shreveport at this point, but instead it's forcing me to sit. Fine; I need to digest anyway.

When I arrived, my only focus was to get some food in me, and then seeing Roy on TV was a major distraction—turns out it was a distraction from the feeling that I won't be leaving so easily. When I started planning my escape I realized my butt was glued to the seat.

Of course, I'm in no rush to run off and get murdered, so I stay. My instincts say I should be fighting whatever it is Fate seems to have planned for me, but logic says that as long as I'm not getting any closer to Shreveport, my chance of survival can only increase every minute I sit here and wait.

And apparently, I am waiting for Maggie.

The door opens and she walks in, straight to me, tossing her backpack onto the seat and plopping down across the table with a heavy sigh.

"Yup," she says. "I kinda suspected this would happen."

fourteen

"WHAT ARE YOU . . . I mean, I thought—" I'm too stunned to complete a sentence.

Maggie waves me off. "Yeah, yeah. Same here. Trust me, I got on the bus for Biloxi, but the loop decided I should end up here." She pulls a french fry off my plate. "Hey, wait. What are *you* doing *here*?"

I push the fries toward her, part of me *very* curious about what happened since she left New Orleans, and part of me knowing that it doesn't really matter—if the loop wanted her to be here with me, that's where the loop would put her.

"I was starving and figured it couldn't hurt to hop off early and grab a bite to eat," I say. "I thought Alexandria was close enough, and I wasn't excited to plant myself in Shreveport if I didn't have to. I mean, if *you* were a couple hundred miles east of here, like you were *supposed* to be, it shouldn't make a difference if I was here or a few miles north."

"Good point." Maggie grabs another fry, then nods at the remnants. "I thought you didn't have any money, Ben. How were you going to pay for this?"

I shrug. "Figured I'd worry about that when the time comes. I know, it doesn't make sense, but I went ahead and ordered anyway. Not something I'd normally do, believe me. But I was *starving*."

"Interesting. I only had a couple of bucks left an hour ago. But now we have this."

She pulls a crisp twenty-dollar bill from her pocket and lays it on the table. "It seems Fate wants to make sure we're well fed."

"Where'd that come from?"

"Would you believe a random donation from a Good Samaritan?"

I pick the bill up and turn it over in my hand. "Is it just me, or is the loop kind of . . . smart?"

"I don't know about smart. *Determined*, though. She does seem determined."

I squeeze some more ketchup onto the plate. "Well, one thing seems pretty clear."

"And what's that?" Maggie asks.

"*She* doesn't want us apart. We get on buses running in opposite directions and still manage to end up having dinner together just a few hours later."

I begin to ask how that went down exactly, but I don't

need to bother. I know the answer—things just *happened*. Fate wants what Fate wants.

Maggie stops a passing waitress and motions for the check. "You're right. That was the first time we've been apart, ever. Every cycle, we've always stuck together until the end. And I don't know that we're strong enough not to work as a team. I mean, if we're just going to keep getting pulled back to each other, we might as well accept it and work together."

I roll my eyes. "Jeez. You don't have to sound so excited."

"What do you mean?"

"'Might as well accept it'? Come on, it's not like our sticking together is a nightmare or anything." Maggie never implied that she'd rather be on her own up to now, and I guess that probably isn't how she meant it to sound. But it surprised me, how it hurt to hear her say it that way.

She gasps. "No, I'm sorry, I just—you know what I mean, right? I definitely like being with you way more than being *without* you; I was just saying that if it's our only option, then we should use it to our advantage. That's all."

"You'd rather be with me than be on your own?"

"Of course. Believe it or not, I like having you around, Ben."

"I like having you around, too," I say.

Maggie laughs and winks as she grabs another fry off my plate.

fifteen

After finishing off the last of my fries, Maggie pays the check with the twenty and stuffs the change into her backpack. "Not much left, but at least we won't be hungry for a while."

We step outside into the night, and a calm breeze brushes between us, the air finally a comfortable temperature. There are only a few cars out on the main road, and it feels as though we have the town to ourselves. I feel like I could stand on this sidewalk forever, the amber streetlights casting Maggie's face in gold and her eyes reflecting the neon signs in the restaurant's window.

But the loop takes advantage of my distraction and nudges me along the side of the building and into the parking lot behind the diner. My body works on its own, feet marching left-right-left-right through the alley while my mind debates whether to fight it or see it through.

My instinct is to resist, but I'm curious. Maggie follows along, apparently curious, too.

Halfway down the alley, we find ourselves standing next to a silver Volkswagen Jetta. Maggie walks around to the driver's side and peers through the window.

"Benjamin . . ."

"Mmm?" I'm watching her hair move in the breeze.

"The keys are in it."

This odd fact snaps me back into focus. "I don't like it. Too convenient."

Maggie doesn't seem to share my skepticism. "Hear me, Ben? The keys are in it. And"—she opens the door—"it's unlocked."

I rush over and shut the door as quietly as I can. "Jeez, Mags, somebody's gonna see."

"Then we'd better hurry."

"What—seriously? Steal a car? I can't believe I'm even saying the words *steal a car*."

Maggie takes my hand and leads me to a dark corner of the lot, away from the lights of the diner. "Listen to me. We need to get ourselves away from Shreveport. We keep getting dragged closer and closer, and I can feel us getting pulled there still. We have no money and only one option."

"The option feels like a trap, Maggie. Remember what Steve said? That the loop will always find a way to get us back on track?" The nervous feeling in my gut tells me I'm on to something. "I don't like it."

"I don't like it, either. But would you feel better staying here, so close to Shreveport, or doing something, anything, to get farther away?" Maggie pauses. "I just don't feel like we're safe here."

I feel it, too. It's dark and unfamiliar, and the closer we are to Shreveport, the stronger Fate's pull seems. And she's right—I would feel better *doing* something than waiting around hoping for things to work out.

"Okay, I agree, but come on—steal a car?"

Maggie points over my shoulder at the Jetta. "Steal *this* car."

"I can't believe I'm even considering this."

"I can't force you to do it, and to be honest, I don't even want you involved if you really don't think it's our best option. You shouldn't do it against your will. But Ben, don't take too long to decide. This window is only open for so long."

I sit on the pavement, pebbles digging into my backside, resting my head in my hands. She made some good points. But really, am I a car thief? I can't go to jail.

But then again, we already *are* wanted for attempted murder, so what's a little grand theft auto on top of it?

It sure would be nice to point the car where we want and just *go*, just get as far away as we can. And if it means saving our lives, saving Maggie's life—

I stand up and brush myself off. "Is it an automatic? Because I can't drive a stick."

sixteen

And now we're somewhere on I-49, headed back home to New Orleans because we don't know where else to go. Even though we're wanted by the cops and can't go near any of our usual haunts (never mind our homes and families), the idea of seeing New Orleans again is comforting.

We haven't been driving very long—maybe forty minutes. Maggie is staring out the window into the night, just spacing out. Her eyelids creep lower and lower, and she yawns at least once a mile. But whenever I suggest that she try to sleep a little, she tells me she's fine and offers to drive.

Now she proves how awake she is by playing with the radio, clicking around the stations and looking through the CDs in the backseat.

"I wish I'd brought my iPod," she says. "All the discs back there are for learning French."

"Très ennuyeux," I say.

"Next time," she says, "we steal a car with satellite radio."

I have a hard time keeping my eyes on the road. For the first time since we met at the mall, we don't have decisions to make, cops to outrun, or fear to neutralize. We do need to keep a low profile, being in a stolen car and everything, but I allow myself to focus on something other than the loop—and naturally my thoughts turn to Maggie.

I'm stealing glances her way, timing them with the glow from the lights that wash over her, lighting her face up for just a second before she's covered again in darkness. I'm wondering if I could put my hand on hers without getting shot down, but I chicken out before even giving it a try.

It's funny how we're so connected, stuck together by Fate like magnets, yet Maggie hasn't shown any real interest in me beyond those two seconds of flirting back at the Mission.

I'm pretty sure she knows I keep looking at her, but I'm starting to not care.

And I'm just beginning to think that everything may be all right, that we've broken free from the loop and it's smooth sailing from here, when it all goes to hell.

It starts with headlights. The wide, bright headlights of a tractor-trailer that cross the median and suddenly flash our way. The van in front of us swerves left, and the tractor-trailer veers right to avoid the collision, sliding to a stop fifty yards away, sprawled across all four lanes.

Me, I'm doing seventy and have no chance of stopping before we skid under the back end of that trailer, which will no doubt turn the Jetta into a convertible and lop off our heads in the process.

Maggie stifles a scream and braces herself, pushing her feet against the floor, pressing her back deep into the seat.

I spin the wheel hard toward the median, and we both jerk to the right. Maggie's head hits her window, and mine feels like it's ready to fly right off. I grip the wheel to keep myself in my seat, and for a second I wonder if this is how an astronaut feels training in a centrifuge.

The g-force releases me, and I pull myself upright. Somehow we bounce across the median in one piece and swing into the northbound lanes, just missing a Toyota Camry that didn't see us until we were inches apart.

Coming up fast in the rearview mirror is a pickup truck, and I stomp the gas pedal hard to the floor. The little VW engine roars and we get up to speed in a blink, and in seconds we're cruising in the center lane as though nothing had happened.

"Shit!" Maggie covers the side of her head with her hand. "At least I didn't break the window."

"Let me see," I say. Maggie turns to face me, and I can already see a bump starting to form where she's pulled her hair back. I run the back of my hand over it, and she winces.

"Oh. Sorry," I say.

"Don't apologize," she says. "We'd be corpses if you didn't get all NASCAR like that. You saved us both."

We sit in silence for a few minutes, bands of amber light passing over us at every streetlight that goes by. On the other side of the highway, we can see traffic already backing up, blocked by the sideways semi. My hands are still trembling from the close call, and the color has left Maggie's face.

In all the excitement, it doesn't occur to either of us for a good five minutes that we've been turned around and are now driving north. Headed straight for Shreveport.

seventeen

I DON'T REALIZE HOW QUIET IT'S BEEN, or for how long, until a single fat raindrop slaps the windshield, making us both jump. The drop nails the middle of the glass and starts spreading, little transparent tentacles reaching out from the center as two more drops splatter, then five, then twenty, and soon it's a thousand all at once.

The rain pounds the hood, windshield, and roof until it's so loud I can barely make out Maggie's words when she says, "This is insane. . . . Better pull over, Ben."

The rain is so heavy that we're only going about fifteen miles an hour as it is, and even at this speed I can't see the lines on the road or the taillights of the car in front of me. Everything beyond the glass looks like liquid marble, swirls of gray and black flowing downward.

I'm looking for the shoulder but can't see more than a few feet ahead. I ease the Jetta to the right, figuring I'll spot a guardrail or something when I get there.

Wrong.

I can tell by the sudden bumps that we're not on pavement anymore. Must be grass. I give up trying to navigate in the downpour and pull off onto the shoulder and put the car in park. I turn off the engine and flip on the hazards.

The wind picks up, and I don't mean a quick breeze or a little puff. Out of nowhere, major gusts hit the car, and we can feel it rock from the force. The rain starts falling more sideways than straight down, and soon there are leaves and twigs falling too.

Through the downpour, we can just make out a sign about twenty feet away, a green rectangular one, and it's twisting, fighting against the wind to stay upright. Always a sucker for the underdog, I'm really rooting for it. And just as it looks like it's about to be torn from the ground, it bounces back and twists some more.

The sign survives and becomes more visible as the rain slowly lets up, and a few cars begin to appear, rolling by on the highway. I start the engine and give the wipers a minute to clear the leaves off the windshield before pulling back onto the pavement. It's still raining hard, but at least now we can see a few car lengths ahead.

I'm wondering if the loop made it rain, or if it was just a storm because, well, storms happen.

"You realize we're pointed north right now, right?" Maggie

asks. "That sign we were watching said 'Shreveport' and had an arrow pointing right to where we're headed."

I hadn't realized it. In hindsight, it was obvious, but my focus had been on keeping the car on the road.

"We should take the next exit," Maggie says. "Figure out where we are and get ourselves pointed south again."

She's right. I turn off at the next exit and pull into the parking lot of a gas station at the end of the ramp.

"I'll run in and find out what town this is," I say, and jog through the rain to the door of the service island.

The middle-aged man behind the counter has a huge mustache that makes him look like a walrus. He greets me silently with a slow-motion blink.

"Hey, I'm trying to get pointed south, toward New Orleans, but the highway is totally jammed up from an accident up the road. Can you tell me the best route to follow until the traffic clears up on I-49?"

Another slow-motion blink. "You want what, now?"

"We're trying to get to New Orleans. But the highway is shut down."

The walrus takes a folded map off the rack behind him and pushes it across the counter. "Three fifty."

"Sorry?"

Blink. "Read a map, son. Three fifty."

Back in the car, I show Maggie the map. "The guy in there was an ass," I say. "Wouldn't give me directions, just sold this to me for our last few bucks."

Maggie sighs and spreads the map over the dash. "Not like

we could buy much with what we had left, anyway."

In the glow of the parking lot floodlights we realize where we are.

"Seriously? We've only gone *that* far?" Maggie has her finger about an inch south of Alexandria. "That's what, twenty miles? We drove for that long and we're only twenty miles south of where we started?"

"Looks like it." I study the map and then gaze through the window, pretending the squiggles and numbers on the map make sense. "So we should be going . . . *that* way?" I point behind us.

From the car, we get a glimpse of the highway, and it's a parking lot as far down as we're able to see. Definitely not an option if we're hoping to actually *get* anywhere.

"What do you think, Mags?"

Maggie shakes her head, wincing. "I don't know. We could get on the highway and sit in traffic for the rest of the night, which isn't too bad since we still wouldn't be in Shreveport, but—"

"But you'd feel better if we were actually putting miles behind us and moving in the other direction."

"That's what I was thinking, yeah."

I agree. The closer we are to Shreveport, the stronger we feel Fate pulling us there. Every inch farther south we can get is a little piece of victory.

Maggie finds a rural route that follows the highway more or less, and we decide to go with that. She jumps out of the car and opens my door, pushing me over into the passenger seat. Before I know it, she's driving and I'm navigating.

Of course, by *navigating,* I mean I'm pointing a flashlight at the map and not letting on that I don't know if I'm even looking at the right state.

"I like the way this car handles," Maggie says. "It corners like a dream. Or so is my understanding from what I've seen in the commercials." This she says after mixing up the levers for the turn signal and wipers three times before even pulling out.

"And you're comparing this to . . . all those other cars you've driven, right? How many is that?"

"Well, none. But it *is* nice, Ben. You don't have to be an experienced driver to know that this is a quality automobile."

It's hard not to smile, even though I'm a little worried that she'll be getting the two of us killed at any moment. She's heavy on the gas and so far has yet to prove that she even *knows* where the brake is. But she's funny and beautiful, and I suppose if I have to die, I'd rather it be by her insanely reckless driving than by being shot. I mean, it all pretty much boils down to the same outcome anyway. Right?

eighteen

IT'S BEEN TEN MINUTES of speeding along this back road, no light at all except our headlights. No moon, no streetlights, nothing but pitch-black inky night.

We're actually making headway, and we're far enough out of the loop that the sick feeling doesn't get to us.

But of course, the moment that I think it, the very second that I realize we're really getting somewhere, it happens again.

We barrel around a tight bend in the road and suddenly we're bathed in blinding light. White flood lamps on tall metal tripods, blue and white spinning lights on the roofs of police cars, white and red lights from an ambulance. My pupils can't dilate fast enough to keep the brightness from being completely overwhelming.

Maggie stops the car behind a police cruiser, pulling up

close enough so our license plate isn't visible. "Hold on a sec," she says, and steps out into the whirling red and white glare.

She talks to the cops for a few minutes, then returns to the car. "Good news and bad news," she says as she pulls her seat belt back on.

I swallow hard. "I'll take the good news first, assuming the bad news isn't that we just got busted for stealing this car."

"Hmm. Well, there's no real good news. I was just trying to soften the blow."

"Soften the blow?"

"Yeah. This accident is going to take at least until morning to clear off the road. We only have one option."

I knew it. I just *knew* it. "We have to go back the way we came."

"Yup. Cop says there's no detour, no side roads from here to get us around the accident. Back the way we came and then take another road near that gas station to get us headed south again."

"You've got to be kidding."

"Sorry, Romeo. But hey, it's only ten minutes wasted, right? Could be worse."

I know full well that it could be worse. What is worrying me is that the loop is just not going to give an inch.

"What if we went back to Alexandria, spent the night there?" Maggie asks. "Maybe catch some Z's in a parking lot or something . . ."

I stare out at the dark blur rushing by my window. "That

would mean we'd be driving north. Past that gas station and toward Shreveport. You cool with that?"

Maggie is silent. I know what she's thinking. There are a million ways we could fly right past Alexandria and move on to our meet-up with Roy.

"I guess we should go back a little ways and try to get around this accident. Alexandria just feels like too much of a risk. Tempting as a good night's sleep may be."

"Okay," I say. "But I drive."

"You're on. And I say we still look for a spot to get some rest. If we find a safe place to park for the night, we should grab it."

I nod.

"It'll be fun, Ben. We'll have a slumber party, just the two of us."

Sold!

nineteen

WE MAKE IT BACK to the gas station and drive just a little way past it before we find the road the cop told Maggie about. Somehow, it's twice as dark and winding as the last one we were on.

"Just a little farther, I think," Maggie says. "There's supposed to be a turn on our left. We take that for a while and that should get us around the accident."

I strain to see beyond the glow of the headlights, wishing we had a GPS or sonar or something to find this turnoff she's talking about. There's now a layer of mist over the road that keeps visibility down to fifty yards or so.

We roll over the bumps and bends in the pavement. The fog thickens, turns dense as milk, but even though we're only doing twenty-five, we still lock up the brakes and skid to a stop when we see a fallen tree across the road.

"You're joking," Maggie says.

No joke. There it is, right in the middle of the last possible route south. It looks as if it was knocked down during the storm, all tangled in power lines and lying sideways. I don't know if it's an oak or a willow or what, but it's huge and there's no way around it.

"Do you get the feeling," Maggie says, "that we could take a thousand different back roads to get south and there would be a thousand different roadblocks between here and home?"

"Mags, I'd be surprised if the loop let us get half an inch closer to home than we are now."

We sit in the fog for a few minutes, silent, thinking about our next move.

"We can turn around and look for another route," I say, "but I think we know what the outcome will be. And I don't know about you, but I can't do this all night. I need some sleep."

Maggie nods. "I'm with you. Sleep. I mean, we may not be getting closer to home, but if we're sleeping, at least we're not any closer to Shreveport."

I back the car up about a quarter mile, until we find a little spot off the side of the road where we can park. It's just on the outside of a curve, but I figure with the fog as thick as it is, anyone driving along this road will be going at a crawl and we'll be visible enough.

Maggie yawns. "Dinnertime."

She reaches into the backseat and grabs her backpack,

rooting around inside until she comes out with a bottle of water and one of the MREs we took from the Mission.

"Hope you're hungry," she says. "One chicken enchilada with sauce, coming up."

She hands me the box, and I thumb open the top flap, dumping everything onto the dash. There's something edible in a brown plastic pouch, something edible in a green plastic pouch, a plastic bag with utensils, salt and pepper, a squeezy-thing of peanut butter, and a package of crackers.

Maggie sifts through the pile. "Damn, I was hoping for Fig Newtons. Sometimes for the dessert you'll get Newtons. I love those things."

I pick up each item and turn it over in my hands. Most of them make sense, but for the life of me I can't figure out how they fit an enchilada into that little package.

"It's kind of cool," Maggie says. "This is how it works." She takes the green pouch, tears the top open, and pours a little water from her bottle into it, then folds the top over and stuffs it back into the cardboard box. The pouch of enchilada goes into the box with it, and she sets it on the dash.

"Now we give it a few minutes to cook. In the meantime"—she rips open the crackers and squeezes some peanut butter on one—"we'll have hors d'oeuvres."

As we eat the crackers, the box on the dashboard starts hissing away, steam escaping in a tiny white jet from one corner. I have no clue how adding plain water to anything can make it hot, but that's why I'm having a military surplus meal in a parked car and not making a living as a nuclear physicist.

I pick up a tiny white packet. "Instant coffee? I could totally go for a cup of coffee right now."

"Not that stuff. I tried it once; it was by far the worst thing I've ever put in my mouth."

"Ah. I see why they give you so much powdered creamer and sugar to go in it."

Maggie laughs. "Not enough, though."

We open the enchilada and share it, doing our best to ignore what it looks like. It's hot, and with my eyes closed, it doesn't taste too bad, but there's something rubbery in there that gives me the creeps, and I'm pretty sure it's *not* the chicken.

"So, Chef Benjamin, how would you have improved this meal?"

I try to figure out what it would have taken to make that meal better, and it's one of the few times I'm genuinely beaten. I suppose some fresh cilantro and a decent hot sauce would help, but at its core the food that came out of that box is just . . . unfixable. Food should have soul, and it seems MREs are born without.

"Honestly? I would have left it back at the Mission and eaten roadkill instead."

Maggie smiles. "Mmm. Possum-tastic."

"Armadi-licious."

The leftovers and packaging all go back in the box, and Maggie tosses it into the backseat. "Totally unsatisfying," she says, and puts her seat back as far as it will go, and I do the same.

It's strange and quiet, the two of us lying back like this,

staring up at the map lights and the switch for the sunroof.

"The good news," Maggie says, "is that it would have happened by now. If we'd been in Shreveport, we'd have been killed earlier tonight."

I give an involuntary shudder, but I'm relieved. From this point on, every minute should feel like a bonus. And then I realize: if our loop always led to us being murdered at nine thirty tonight, but it's now—well, I don't know what time it is *exactly*, but I know it's well after eleven—we're not in the loop anymore. We've outlived it. I think.

"Are we home free?" I ask. "I mean, we've beaten it, right? We stayed out of Shreveport and the loop had scheduled us to be killed a couple hours ago, but we're still here. So . . . we made it. Didn't we?"

Maggie shakes her head. "Ben, if you've jinxed us I'm going to kick your ass."

"I'm just saying, I think we pulled it off. Don't you?"

Maggie settles into a relaxed smile, one I haven't seen up to now. "I do."

I slide down a little more into my seat, getting comfortable. The sick feeling in my gut is gone, although the antique military-grade Mexican food I ate a few minutes ago is threatening to make trouble.

"You know, it's pretty amazing," Maggie says. "All the trips through the loop we've made, you and I have never been a day older than we are right now. That's big." She stares soberly at the liner of the roof. "We've never been this old before."

"We should celebrate," I say.

"Whatcha have in mind, Romeo?"

I shrug. "No idea. But it's a pretty special occasion, right? We're the oldest we've ever been? Sounds like a big deal to me."

Maggie nods. "True. But then again, for pretty much everyone else, they can say that every second of the day and they'd be right. 'I've never been older than I am right now.'"

"You know we're not like everyone else, though, Mags."

"No, we're not. So—" She turns to face me. "A party, then? With a DJ? Maybe pony rides and a clown, too?" She's smirking.

"You're making fun of me."

"No, I'm—" She pauses. "Yeah, you're right. I totally am. Sorry." Her smirk turns to a wide smile, and her eyes sparkle in the faint light of the dash. She takes both my hands in hers and lifts her chin resolutely. "So let's party, Benjamin."

Maggie turns on the radio, clicking through the stations until she hits a song she likes. I've heard it before; it's new and catchy and has a great beat, though I couldn't tell you who sings it if my life depended on it. Luckily, naming the artist who recorded this song is one of the few things my life has *not* depended on today.

She turns the volume way up and gets out of the car, taking a spot a few yards away in the wash of the headlights. She grins, waiting for me, dragging me out of the car with that special power that girls have over boys, the ability to control men like puppets and make them do whatever a girl wants. I open my door and climb out despite the rising terror at the realization that I may have to dance.

The headlights make solid beams in the fog, cones of white that blaze from the car's grille, and fade to nothingness in the dark. "Wait," I say, and reach back into the car and turn the hazard lights on. Now there's a pulsing amber light radiating through the mist. It's a pretty cool effect.

Maggie's hips twitch and she beckons me closer, her shoulders moving to the music. She laughs, and I can't tell if it's from the silliness of the situation or in anticipation of seeing me try to dance. I silently pray that the rain will start again so we have to get back in the car.

She stops swaying and puts on a cartoonish frown. "What? Does Benjamin not dance?"

"No, he doesn't. But he's perfectly happy staying right here." I lean against the hood and smile my best smile, hoping that will be the end of it.

Maggie walks to me, the fog swirling around her in the headlights, and takes my hand. "Come on, Ben. We're having a party and you're *going* to dance."

She leads me a few yards away, where the light isn't so harsh and the blinking amber hazards fall softly on her face. I've never seen a girl look so beautiful, and it almost paralyzes me. I don't think I could dance if I wanted to.

Just as she takes both of my hands and is ready to shame me into some horrible, twitching indignity, the song ends, fading into another. The tempo bottoms out to a slow, dreamy beat, and Maggie's body slows to match the rhythm. She lets go of my hands, and for a moment I panic, unsure of what I'm supposed to do with them. But she slips her fingers around my back, wrapping her arms under mine, and holds me to her tightly, her head resting against my shoulder.

I put my arms around her and let her move me, swaying slowly, almost imperceptibly. I figure I'm supposed to *lead* in this dance, but I know better than to deliberately mess with things when they're going so perfectly.

"You're a good dancer," she says quietly.

"Because I haven't fallen down yet?"

"Because right now I don't want to be anywhere else."

I have no response to that. Any words that come to mind are just filler, clichés to kill the silence. I keep my mouth shut, deciding that staying quiet is preferable to whatever stupid thing I'd come up with. So I squeeze her a little more, and she squeezes back, and I just stare into the fog, grinning like a fool.

The song ends and cross-fades into an upbeat song, the world of top-forty pop breaking into our reality, trespassing in our little world of soft misty light and slow dances. Maggie doesn't seem to be in the mood for a party anymore, and smiles sweetly, giving me one last squeeze. "Thanks for dancing with me," she says. "Party over?"

I'm in desperate need of sleep and can't believe I've made it this far without embarrassing myself, so I nod in agreement. "It was a nice party," I say sheepishly.

Back in the car, my thoughts turn to all we've been through in such a short time, and how we may have gotten ourselves free of the loop. And while we still are wanted by the cops and face a world of trouble when we get back to New Orleans, the thought that we may not be counting the hours to our deaths is exhilarating.

"I really enjoyed not getting murdered with you tonight, Ben."

"I enjoyed not getting murdered with you, too," I say.

I can't help it. I smile. Then Maggie smiles. And pretty soon we're laughing at nothing other than each other's laughter and the idea that we've escaped our loop, and I feel her hand tentatively brush against my arm. Her fingers touch my forearm and stay there, and I swear my core temperature rises by ten degrees.

"Ben?" she says.

"Yeah."

"If it doesn't work out for us, you know, I've had way more fun this trip through the loop than I've ever had before. It really has been different this time, and I just wanted to say that if we die tonight, or tomorrow—well, I can't wait to meet you again on the escalator."

I still feel warm all over, but now my heart is racing. Maggie's hand slips down my arm and past my wrist, and before I have time to do something stupid and ruin it, we are holding hands.

I'm afraid to breathe for fear of doing something to change how perfect this moment is. Instead, I lie completely still; I'm not ready to fall asleep, but my eyes are burning and I have to close them.

I run my thumb over the back of Maggie's hand—it's soft, and she gives me a light squeeze. I think that if I'm going to die, now would be a good time. Right now, holding hands, neither of us hungry or scared, just grateful to be together.

I fight off sleep with everything I have.

twenty

I KNOW IT'S A DREAM, but I can't wake myself from it.

I am alone in the middle of the mall parking lot, crouching between two cars, and I can feel Roy's presence. I put my head to the asphalt and look between the wheels of the SUV in front of me, watching for his feet. I can hear his footsteps echoing across the expanse of pavement, no other sound but the scrape of his shoes as he comes closer and closer. Still, I can't see him.

I turn my head and look through the wheels of the car behind me, then between the wheels of the next car over, and the next. Black half-moons, the silhouettes of tires against the pavement crowd together as I watch the bright shapes between them for Roy's shoes.

Nothing.

I get to my feet and try to see through the windows beyond the SUV, but there are too many obstructions. I have no clear view and the footsteps are coming closer.

When he speaks, Roy's voice sounds close enough to be right in my ear. It's barely above a whisper, a raspy whine that slithers out of him and is meant only for me.

"The game is over, Benjamin. You're wasting your time. *Our* time."

The parking lot is now empty. I crouch alone, exposed, in the center of the lot. The sun has set, and two lights on poles that reach high into the air illuminate the pavement, casting crisp circles of amber light below. One of the circles is centered on me, like I am an actor in a spotlight on a darkened stage.

The other circle of light reveals Roy. He stands tall, straight, strong. He grins, and the glow from the light above casts his face in eerie shadows, the green of his eyes gleaming like emeralds. The light makes his nose look long and sharp, his chin drawing to a point, eyebrows arched.

I try to stand, but cannot. It's as though there are sandbags on my shoulders pinning me down, the weight almost forcing me onto my back. I huddle down in a tiny ball.

"You looked frightened, Benjamin. You don't like this game? All kids love games. Come on, let's play."

I can't speak.

Roy takes a step toward me, and the light follows him, keeping him dead in the center. "You can't possibly win this game. You are playing against *me*. You're playing against destiny. I *am* destiny, Benjamin. I am unbeatable."

He takes another three steps forward, and as the light moves with him, it reveals Maggie, now standing in the circle with Roy. Her head hangs low, her shoulders slumped, and a tear has rolled down her cheek, leaving a glistening trail.

She lifts her eyes until they meet mine, and she says, "I'm sorry, Ben."

At her words, Roy's smile grows, his mouth spreading impossibly wide. The pointed edges of his grin creep almost to his ears.

"Say good-bye, Benjamin." He draws a gun from his back pocket—large, polished nickel. He places it to Maggie's head, just above her ear. "Don't worry, you'll see her again. And you'll see me, too. Every two days until forever comes, Benjamin. You'll see me blow your precious Maggie's head off over and over, until forever comes."

The corners of his mouth have now moved all the way up to his ears, and he pulls his lips back to show off his teeth, a seemingly endless row of stark white pearls. He drops his lower jaw and laughs, a low mocking cackle that echoes off the asphalt and fades into the darkness. His mouth opens wider and wider, his laughter louder and louder, until it rings in my head like the blast of a car horn. His jaws open wide enough to drop a basketball in.

Then the laughter turns into a scream, a deafening squeal.

My eyes pop open, and hot white lights blind me, tearing through my corneas.

Instinctively, I throw my hands in front of my face. On

some level, I'm aware that I'm in the car with Maggie, but somehow the sight of the steering wheel in front of me only adds to my confusion.

The scream and the lights. That's all. Not even a full second. And then everything goes black.

twenty-one

Now there's a flashlight in my eyes, tiny but focused and bright. Noises, all around me, insistent voices and the slamming of car doors. Maybe truck doors, solid and heavy. More lights, red and white, spinning across the trees in front of me. A man's voice to my right: "This one's not responsive."

I tilt my head to the right and look over my shoulder. I'm lying on the grass, and a few yards away I see a man in a dark uniform kneeling next to Maggie. Her eyes are closed, and the man is listening to her heart. Her right hand lays open, palm up, as though waiting for me to grasp it. The light seems to dim and everything sparkles, then blackness creeps in.

• • •

Another flash. Fluorescent lights this time, rows of them overhead. Nurses in brightly colored scrubs, yellow painted walls, the smell of disinfectant. I feel like I'm pinned down, lying on a cot maybe, but realize it's only a blanket and sheet on me. Still, it feels like it's made of lead. I must be tucked in tight.

Someone's squeezing my finger, but when I look to see who it is, I find it's just a little plastic clamp with a wire that goes to a bank of computers next to my bed. All the screen shows are lists of numbers, some blinking, some not. A blue curtain hangs from a track in the ceiling, splitting the room in half.

I don't hear anyone on the other side. I figure I must be alone.

A nurse wakens me with a tray of food. Something is not right, though I can't place what it is. It feels like the middle of the night. There are no windows, so I can't even see if it's dark out. I know I slept—did I sleep a whole day and it's night again? But then I'm being fed what I'm guessing is breakfast, judging by the little cup of orange juice on the tray. My internal clock must be off.

The nurse puts the tray on a table next to the bed and swings it over me so I can sit up and eat. I'm not hungry, but even if I were, I doubt I'd be excited by what's lurking under those plastic covers on the tray. It smells vaguely food-related but not much like food itself. Like disinfectant with a touch of burned toast.

The nurse nods encouragingly at one of the dishes and says, "Flapjacks this morning. Give 'em a shot." I look at the tray and find three tan pancake-shaped sponges with a square of cold butter atop each one. The nurse smiles awkwardly and returns to the food cart in the hall to inflict her culinary horror on the occupant of the next room.

I peel back the plastic on the pancakes, but the smell of food makes my stomach flip. I push it aside. I'm *definitely* thirsty, though.

There's a pitcher and an empty glass next to my bed. But as I lean to pour a cup, a bolt of pain rips through my right side. The sudden pain makes me gasp and jerk my arm back, my hand knocking the cup off the nightstand.

The same nurse pops her head in. "Is everything okay in here? I thought I heard— Oh honey, you dropped your cup. Here you go."

She puts a new cup on the nightstand. "Well, how are we feeling?"

I'm sure *we* are feeling just great, but *I* have a pain in my side like there's a spear stuck in it, and my head spins when I try to sit up. Not to mention the overall sensation, as though someone beat every inch of me with a sack of bricks while I slept.

"I'm okay. Thirsty."

The nurse pours some water into the cup. "I bet you're pretty sore, huh."

I nod. "I don't even know what happened. The last thing I remember is falling asleep in the car with—"

I freeze.

Maggie.

I start to sit up and slide one leg off the bed, pushing the sheet and blanket off of me, and the pain in my chest almost makes me scream. I bite my lip and push myself up on one hand, but the nurse has a good grip on my shoulder and eases me back down.

"You stay put, kiddo," she says. "If you think it hurts now, wait until that broken rib of yours pierces a lung because you wouldn't sit still."

"But—" I push back against the nurse's hand and try to sit up. "Maggie."

"Oh." The nurse turns and looks over her shoulder, seemingly through the heavy curtain that divides the little room. "Your friend."

"Yes! Is she okay?"

"I suppose she's about as well off as you are. It's a miracle either of you survived, from what I heard. Apparently, that little Volkswagen you were in looked like it'd gone through the crusher. More of a cube than a car. Medics had to cut it to pieces just to get the two of you out."

So, there it is: we were hit by another car while we slept.

"And it sure didn't help that you were out in the middle of nowhere like that. They had to drive you ten minutes north just to find a place for the chopper to land."

"Chopper?" I don't remember being on a helicopter.

"Oh, sure. They thought you might have had some bleeding in here"—she points to her forehead—"which is nothing to joke about. Put you both on the chopper and flew you here to make sure you got taken care of properly."

I swallow hard, afraid to ask. "And where is . . . *here*?"

"Home of the best care anywhere," she says, smiling wide. "You're on the fourth floor of the Hospital of Greater Shreveport."

twenty-two

WE WERE AT LEAST a two-hour drive south of here, parked, even *asleep*—and we still end up in Shreveport? What the *hell.*

"Ben." Maggie's voice slips through the blue curtain.

I exhale like I've been holding my breath for days, and sink back into my mattress, relieved to know she's awake and talking. Then I sit up as much as I can without whimpering in pain. "Actually, I prefer Benjamin."

I hear her suppressing a laugh.

"You okay, Mags?"

"I think so. I'm hooked up to so much stuff I can hardly move. My head hurts, that's all I know. You?"

I try to sound casual. "I'm all right."

She snorts before saying, "Liar."

I slide off the bed, gritting my teeth, and pull back the curtain. It slides easily along a metal track overhead. "Peekaboo."

Maggie rolls her eyes, making no effort to sit up. There's a wide purple bruise across her right eye, another on her shoulder, and an ugly cut on her bottom lip. And those are only the parts I can *see*. A blanket covers the rest of her.

"Jeez, Maggie. You don't look so hot."

"Thanks, Romeo. I'll remember you said that. Always." Her voice is meek and breathy. "You look a little roughed up yourself."

"Nah, it's just a few bruises." I wave it off.

Maggie rolls her eyes. "A few bruises, my ass."

I try to fake a smile, but a bolt of pain shoots through my chest, and the best I can muster is quivering lips pulled back over clenched teeth. "I'll live. At least long enough to get murdered by Roy."

"Speaking of . . . You know where we are?"

I grimace. "Yeah." My mind is racing in crazy little circles, trying to figure out what everything boils down to. We managed to end up in Shreveport, but did the loop pull us here, or is it just an unsettling coincidence? And what about Maggie? If we still need to face off with Roy, she's in no shape to make it through. Neither am I, for that matter.

I pull the curtain back as far as it will go and sit on the edge of my bed. I watch Maggie watch me, her breathing slow, her eyes heavy. An IV snakes from her left arm to a bag of saline hanging above her. In her condition, I doubt she could fight off a mosquito, never mind the will of the universe.

"It seems like a month ago," I say.

"What does?"

"Us meeting. Running through the mall. Haircuts in the ladies' room. Sleeping at the Mission."

Maggie smiles weakly. "Stealing a car. You little thief, you." Then she turns serious. "We need to get out of here, Ben. Pretty soon they'll figure out who we are when they start looking for insurance cards and parents and stuff."

She's right, as always. We don't know where we stand in the loop, and I'm sure the police would be very happy to have us staying at their place instead of here. We could very well find out that all is fine and forgiven—but I doubt it, and in our shape I'd rather not take any chances. It wouldn't take much to nudge us right back into the cycle and into Roy's lap.

Maggie reads my mind. "Don't worry about a plan yet. Right now we just have to get moving before the cops show up."

She pulls the blanket back slowly, and I can see that every movement is causing her pain. I yank the pulse monitor off my finger and shuffle to her bed to offer some help, each step sending lightning through my chest.

I'm expecting a barrage of protests, but Maggie stays quiet as I hold her hand. She lets me take her weight, and I put my other arm around her back, supporting her.

"We might have a little problem if we find ourselves in a situation where I need to run very far. Or run at all. Or walk." She pulls the last bit of blanket back, and her calf is bandaged from her ankle up to her knee. It looks like the dressing needs to be changed too, as blood has already seeped through parts of it. The unwrapped parts of her leg and foot are splotchy, dark purple.

I put my hand over my mouth and point at her leg, trying not to look. "Jeez, Maggie, what happened *there*?"

She stares at the bandage as though she can see the wound underneath. "I think I was . . . *impaled* by something." She touches the bandage gingerly, making a hissing sound as she inhales sharply through her teeth.

She slides off the edge of the bed until her bare feet touch the floor, taking her time and only putting weight on her good leg. But at least at this point she's standing.

"Oh," she mutters. *"Owie."*

She's run out of slack in the IV line, and has almost pulled the needle out of her arm. It's held in place with tape.

"We'll have to take care of that," I say. I'm not squeamish, but I'm hoping she'll have the guts to pull the needle out herself.

Maggie waves me away and peels the tape off. I can see the needle where it goes into her skin on the inside of her elbow. She looks up at me with a pained expression and grips the catheter with two fingers.

"Here goes nothing," she says.

In a slow but steady pull, she slips the needle out and lets it fall to her side. Her lips are pursed tight and her eyes are wide, but she nods as though it was far less painful than expected.

"Clothes," she says.

I respond with a blank stare, and she snaps her fingers as though waking me from hypnosis. "We're pretty much naked here. I'm sure that's okay with you, Romeo, but I'd feel better in something that at least covers my ass."

She bunches the hospital gown together behind her to demonstrate the point. I turn my head to look, and realize that my own backside has been out there the whole time. Why don't they at least have Velcro to keep these things closed?

With one hand keeping my gown shut behind me, I begin the search for our clothes. Under the bed? Nope. Bathroom? Nope. Ah . . . two large plastic bags on a shelf next to the bedside chair. Rather than hobble across the room, I toss Maggie's bag beside her on the bed. "Just this. Your backpack must still be in the car. Or whatever's *left* of the car."

"Curtain," she says.

I pull the curtain until it splits the room once more, and we start to get out of the hospital gowns and into our clothes. And while on the one hand I'm disappointed the curtain is between us, I'm also relieved that Maggie isn't watching me change. She doesn't need to see me in all my scrawny paleness.

My gown falls to the floor, and I take a quick survey of the cuts and bruises. There aren't too many, but the ones I have are no joke. One bruise on the side of my chest is about the size of a saucer and so tender I can barely touch it. There's another long bruise down the side of my leg, plus a bandage on my left shoulder. I peel the tape back a little and see stitches that sew up a wound two inches long. It's a straight, clean cut. Broken glass, maybe?

Maggie's voice comes though the curtain. "What's the damage, Ben?"

"Just some bruises. A few stitches. Nothing major." I lean down to pick up my bag of clothes, and before I can bite my lip, I bark like a kicked puppy.

Oh yes, the broken rib.

"Sounds like more than a few bruises to me."

I don't bother with a reply; she'll know I'm lying anyway. The stabbing pain in my side reminds me of what the nurse said about my broken rib puncturing a lung if I don't keep still. Great.

The curtain slides open with a *swish,* and there's Maggie, fully dressed. She rolls her eyes and snaps the curtain back again. "Today, Ben."

Perfect. She catches me wearing nothing but a hospital bracelet, standing there like an idiot.

"Don't worry," she says through the curtain. "I didn't see a thing."

"Hey!" I yelp. "What's that supposed to mean?"

twenty-three

I HAVE MY ARM AROUND MAGGIE, propping her up as best as I can without squeezing anything too hard, touching a wound, or just generally causing more pain than she's already in. It's not easy, because I'm limping along pretty awkwardly myself, the pain in my chest blazing like a hot coal stuck between my ribs. And bad as it is, it's still not enough to distract me from all the other pains in my body.

I'm holding up better than Maggie, though. She winces at every step but refuses to stop for a break when I suggest one. She knows we need to get out of this hospital, and do it quickly—the police could be here any minute. Right now we're too beat up to outrun them, and too exhausted to outsmart anybody.

If we had the luxury of time, we could change our look

again, maybe new dye jobs or haircuts for both of us, new clothes from the lost-and-found box. But at the moment we'll be lucky if we can just make it to the exit without being spotted.

Maggie mumbles in my ear. "What floor are we on?"

I glance at the little blue plaque next to the door. It reads: JANITORIAL. And beneath that, *403*.

"Fourth floor," I whisper. "I take it you'd prefer an elevator rather than the stairs?"

Maggie shakes her head. "Cameras in the elevator. Just get me to the top and push me down the stairs."

I know she's making a joke, but it's just not funny without her usual smirk.

We do have a bit of luck going our way, though—there are round security mirrors near the ceiling at each turn in the corridor, to keep gurneys from colliding as they come around the corners. We stop for a breath at each intersection and check the mirrors before moving on. Not that there's a whole lot we could do if we saw a SWAT team approaching.

Maggie spots a sign for the stairs, and gestures weakly. "Take a left, Romeo, we're getting close. And just so we're clear, I was kidding about pushing me down the stairs."

The mirrors at each corner are a big help, but they don't always help us watch our backs. A man's voice over my shoulder startles me.

"You two. I'm going to need to talk to you for a minute."

We freeze. Maggie's gaze moves slowly from the floor to

me—her face registers neither surprise nor fear, just a tired look of resignation.

We turn to face the man behind us, and I nearly let a whimper escape when I see that he's a uniformed police officer. One hand is on the radio microphone by his shoulder, and the other is resting on the grip of his gun. "I need you to come with me, please."

He says *please,* but it's clear he isn't asking. He thumbs the button on his radio's microphone and says, "Tell Lewis I found the two kids, still on the fourth floor. Doubt they're in any shape to have gotten very far anyway."

Maggie walks even more slowly, shoulders slumped, head down. Her hand moves to her stomach, and she moans, "I need to sit."

The officer's eyes narrow as he glances from her face to mine, then he looks quickly in both directions down the hallway for a nurse. "You better not be screwing with me," he says.

Maggie slides from my arms and down to the floor in slow motion, onto her knees, hands clutching her stomach. Her hair falls and covers her face.

"I'll find a nurse," the cop says. "If either of you moves a muscle, there will be trouble."

Maggie nods. I nod, too.

The officer jogs down the corridor and around a corner. Maggie grabs my leg and pulls herself up, at the same time pushing me to start walking. We turn the corner and stumble through the first open doorway we see. I shut the door behind me.

A patient's room. A *sleeping* patient's room at that, which is another good bit of luck—no need to explain our presence. A human-shaped lump lies under the sheets and blanket, the television showing *The Price Is Right.*

There's a wheelchair next to the bed. I grab it, and before Maggie can protest, I push her to sit in it and we're back out the door. Moving much faster now.

Two more corners and we're in sight of both the stairs and the elevator. The stairs seem too slow of a route now that we've been spotted. I'm guessing they would take us three minutes per floor, minimum, if I have to help Maggie down each flight.

Heading to the elevator, we pass by a nurse's station. A white coat hangs on a hook near the phone, the desk unattended.

Luck, luck, luck.

I know I should be wary of *anything* that happens in our favor, but right now I just need to get the two of us off this floor. I grab the coat and pull it on as I wheel Maggie to the elevator.

She chuckles. "Doctor Benjamin, MD."

I'm happy to see a hint of a smirk find its way to the corners of her mouth.

The elevator doors close behind us, and Maggie thumbs the button for the parking garage. We keep our heads down and out of sight of the camera up in the corner.

"Are you okay?" I ask. Maggie's routine with the cop was a little too convincing.

"I'll survive," she says. "But look at you—way to take charge, Dr. Benjamin. You're turning into a real action hero."

My whole face is sore, but it doesn't stop my first honest grin since waking up. Dr. Benjamin, the action hero. I cough and can taste what I'm pretty sure is blood in my mouth.

The doors open on the parking level, and again, luck goes our way. It's completely deserted.

twenty-four

"I DON'T THINK WE'RE GOING to find another car gassed up with the keys in it, Mags."

We're standing in the parking garage, my voice barely above a whisper yet echoing over the concrete. The place is loaded with cars, but I have a feeling that, despite a few turns of good luck, Fate isn't going to let us leave town so easily. Instead, now I'm thinking that she wanted us out of the hospital but not out of town. Every one of these cars is probably locked up a dozen ways with alarms. I wouldn't be surprised if they all had flat tires, too.

Maggie leans against a concrete pillar, exhausted. Her face looks terrible—bruised and bloody—but under the mess she's still beautiful.

Her lip has started bleeding again, and she dabs at it with

the back of her hand. She sighs. "I'm wiped out, Ben."

"I know. I am, too." I stand next to her and help her slide down with her back to the concrete, until we're slouched against the pillar, side by side.

"What now?" she says. "I can't even think straight."

"You just need to sleep. We both do. We'll figure out the next step when we've had a little rest."

Maggie's hand hangs limply at her side, and I put it in mine. The blood she wiped from her lip has dried already, a pale rust color streaked across her perfect tan skin.

Gazing out toward the street, my eye catches a sign: SUPER 8 MOTEL.

"Don't fall asleep yet," I say. "I have an idea for a place we can rest for a little while."

Maggie nods lethargically and puts her arm around my shoulders. I help her to her feet and gasp as another flash of pain streaks through my chest. The pain from the broken rib is dizzying.

It takes us forever to walk out of the parking garage, but once again we get lucky at the exit, because there's no one in sight. We have our arms around each other like newlyweds, and while Maggie's black eye is pretty nasty, her hair falls over it perfectly. As long as we walk slowly we don't look like we need an ambulance. Or a hearse.

I start thinking that if we *are* getting pulled back into the loop, neither of us is in any condition to fight Roy. Mentally and physically, we're already beaten. And I start wondering if the loop would be satisfied if only *one* of us died here, so maybe the other would be let go. Do we both really need to die? Wouldn't one of us be enough?

And while everything seems to have fallen apart—one minute eating nuclear-powered enchiladas in a stolen car and holding hands, laughing over nothing, and the next minute waking up half dead in a hospital a mile away from where we are destined to die—I smile for just a second because my arm is around Maggie and she is leaning on me.

That's the moment that I realize I'm going to die for her.

twenty-five

THE MOTEL IS ONLY TWO BLOCKS AWAY, and we head straight for it. The clock on the sign for the bank across the street says it's ten fourteen a.m. and eighty-four degrees, though in the shadows it feels cooler. But between the lack of sleep earlier and waking in the windowless hospital room after who knows *how* many hours unconscious, my internal clock is totally out of whack. It still seems like the middle of the night to me.

We walk around to the back of the motel. I sit Maggie on the curb outside one of the rooms. A door a few rooms down is open, and I figure housekeeping is probably in there straightening up.

Maggie gestures to the giant Super 8 sign that looms over the parking lot. "This whole thing was your plan to get me into a motel, wasn't it, Romeo? From day one you've been trying to get me so physically and emotionally exhausted that I'll just fall into your arms in a Super 8 in Shreveport."

"No use denying it any longer, I guess."

She starts to smile but winces, and her hand snaps up to the bruise around her eye. "Don't make me smile anymore. It hurts my face."

I stretch my legs—the only part of my body that doesn't ache—out in front of me. "Why do you always call me that?"

"Call you what?"

"Romeo."

Maggie eases herself down until she's lying on her back in the shade of the building's eaves. "It's not obvious?"

"Not to me."

"You're telling me you've never read *Romeo and Juliet*?"

"Of course I *read* it. I'm just too tired to *remember* any of it at the moment." In reality, I pretty much skipped the whole thing when it was assigned reading last year.

Maggie sighs. "Okay. Well, Romeo and Juliet were what Shakespeare called *star-crossed*, right? 'Star-crossed lovers.' It means they were drawn together but their relationship was doomed from the start. Like us. We didn't *choose* to end up here together; that was just the way it had to happen. And as for the rest, well . . . you have to admit, we do seem pretty doomed."

"I suppose."

"So you're Romeo."

"And you're Juliet?"

She smirks. "Are you trying to be my star-crossed lover, Benjamin?"

I can feel my face getting hot. I imagine it's roughly the same shade of red as a ripe tomato. I look back at the room with the open door, watching the housekeeper's shadow moving along the curtains in the front window. Something about the doorknob keeps bugging me, like it's screaming *LOOK at me!*

I'm looking.

My mind turns to a cop show I saw as a kid, some detective thing my dad used to watch. The doorknob catches my eye again.

Bingo.

I stand up, the pain in my chest burning like a branding iron. "You have any gum?"

Still lying on her back on the sidewalk, Maggie slides a hand into the front pocket of her jeans. "Actually, I do. Here."

She holds up the pack, and I stuff two pieces into my mouth. "I'll be back in a sec, Mags."

She dismisses me with a halfhearted wave, and I do my best nonchalant bystander impression as I stroll toward the room with the open door. Inside, I hear a vacuum.

I give a quick peek through the door and see that the housekeeper has her back to me. I take the gum out of my mouth and jam it into the strike plate—the part that the latch from the doorknob clicks into—then turn back as smoothly as I can and take my seat next to Maggie. I was thinking I'd call her Juliet to get that conversation started again, but she's already managed to doze off.

twenty-six

I WATCH THE DOOR until I see the housekeeper leave, then I help Maggie into the room and lay her on the bed, taking her shoes off and pulling the covers over her. She falls back to sleep even before I pull the curtains shut.

I set the bedside alarm clock for four p.m., stuff it under my pillow, and lie down on the bed next to Maggie, my hands folded over my chest. I breathe in once, out once, and fall asleep.

After what only feels like moments, the alarm buzzes, muffled by the pillow, and I snap the dial over to the OFF position. I roll slowly off the bed, careful not to wake Maggie. She's out cold, her breathing steady and shallow, and I brush her hair away from where it fell over her cheek.

It breaks my heart to leave her here.

• • •

This is so much harder than I thought. I had assumed I could just walk out of the motel, and the loop would steer me to Roy; but what Fate wanted most was for me to be with Maggie. As soon as I leave the room, I can feel the loop pulling me back to her, and that sickness takes over: nausea, a soaking sweat, and pain, as if all my bones are breaking. And I feel like I'm waist-deep in water, walking against a current that's rushing back toward the motel.

I guess it makes sense: In the proper order of things, I meet up with Maggie, *then* we die. Fate just wants to make sure we do things in the right sequence according to plan.

I've pretty much resigned myself to the dying part. Feeling how strong the pull is, and having to fight just to do something as simple as go south instead of north, I've realized now that it's an unwinnable battle. We've fought tooth and nail to be anywhere other than Shreveport, and though we seemed to make headway at times, in the end it made no difference. Here we are, half dead already, in Shreveport.

I'm just hoping that Maggie will stay asleep long enough for me to do what I need to. I'm banking on the idea that if *one* of us goes, it just might be enough for Fate to let her out of the loop. It *has* to be enough—we can't hold Fate off forever, and Maggie's in no condition to fight for herself.

So now I'm trudging away from the motel, trying to focus entirely on tracking down Roy. If I think too much about what will happen when I find him, I'll freak out. Especially if my plan works—because if I break us out of the loop, I don't get to do any of this over. Dead is dead.

I have nothing to go on. No clues, no locations, no idea of where to start looking. I can feel the loop pushing me, trying to send me back to Maggie. I've gotten so used to the feeling that I don't have to burn too much energy to resist. But I sure do feel it.

Think, Benjamin. Where would I be if I were Roy?

I'd be looking for those two kids I'm supposed to kill.

And that happens where?

At the OTB. Off-Track Betting.

Maggie had said that as soon as the money was in our hands Roy would be there at the OTB, waiting for us. It's a start, anyway.

All I have to do is find the local OTB and stake it out. Roy will *have* to be there, waiting for us. But how do I find where to go? What if there's more than one OTB?

I need to get online. . . . Maybe I can find a place that sells computers.

I gaze as far down one end of the street as I can, seeing only the top floors of the hospital, the motel, and a few buildings that are probably just apartments. But the other end of the street holds a miracle: good old Walmart.

In the electronics section I find half a dozen laptops on display, open and running. I slide up to the closest one and open a browser.

More good luck: I'm online.

In the search box, I type *OTB Shreveport* and wait for my answer. How many could there be?

I get ninety-seven thousand results.

I narrow it down a bit with a few more keywords and—ah, that's better. Two locations.

Interesting.

I pull up a map of the area and find that one place is not too far from here—maybe a fifteen-minute walk. The other is three miles, probably an hour away.

This is when my head starts to spin. Which one would Fate want to send me to? I have a good feeling about the one that's close by, but maybe that's just because it's also closer to Maggie. Does that mean that the farther one is where I need to be? Is that where Roy is?

Maybe. But what if Fate *knows* that I'm resisting it, and that I'll probably go against what I'm being pulled toward? Wouldn't she then pull the old reverse-psychology thing and push me toward the *right* one?

I'm going to get a brain hemorrhage if I keep this up. I should just flip a coin.

I dig in my pockets and come up empty.

This is ridiculous.

As I scan the area for any little thing that can help me decide, what do you know—my gaze lands on a shiny quarter at my feet.

Creepy.

I flip the coin, heads being the closer of the OTB places. The quarter lands tails up. Of course. I'm in for a nice long walk in the afternoon sun.

twenty-seven

So I'm thinking I *must* be headed in the right direction, because Fate takes advantage of any opportunity to put something in my way. At every intersection I have to wait forever before traffic will clear enough for me to cross. A power line has fallen across one street, and the sidewalk is closed for the whole block. Someone has conveniently stolen half the street signs along the way, so I'm never really sure I'm even on the right street, and my chest feels like someone is twisting a knife deeper and deeper between my ribs.

A fat, rusty knife.

And I still have the sickness of fighting against the loop to deal with. Sweat runs into my eyes, and my stomach has decided to throw some dry heaves into the mix.

I spend the better part of an hour pushing through the

pain and hobbling down streets that all look alike. Meanwhile, the sun is setting and it's getting harder to find my way. I had to memorize the basic directions since I couldn't print anything off the computer at Walmart, and now I'm not convinced that I'm going the right way anymore.

In fact, the only way that I know I'm headed in the right direction is when another obstacle pops up. Like a three-block detour because a new sidewalk is being poured.

Ah. I must be on track.

It's completely dark by the time I get to the OTB. Inside, yells and cheers erupt out of relative silence, and I think a race must have just been decided. From the signs posted on the door, it's obvious that someone my age is not invited in.

I look through the windows as best as I can, but it's dark in there, and the only thing I can see clearly is a row of television monitors high up on the wall and figures standing frozen in front of the screens. It's too dim to make out any faces, but I can tell that Roy's not in there. Even just the silhouette of him would stand out to me for sure.

I wander along the side of the building and around back, peering between the Dumpsters and parked cars for Roy. Older men stand in the shadows smoking, or are bent over squinting at discarded betting slips in the amber glow of the parking lot lights. I think I'd feel safer in the middle of a prison riot, but then I remember that I'm looking for the man who is destined to kill me—and that perspective makes this place seem pretty tame.

I *really* hope I'm in the right place.

I find a dark shadow by the back fence of the parking lot, take a seat on the curb, and wait for Roy.

After an hour or two, I know I'm in the wrong place. Something would have happened by now. Roy would have showed, or Maggie would have somehow materialized. The most telling sign of all, though, is the sudden feeling that I want to get up and start walking. The loop is pulling me back in, and at this point I'm just too weak to fight it.

But it had given me a rest for a while—I'd sat here without the loop pushing me in any direction at all, until now. So what's changed? Maybe it knows I'm not going back to Maggie no matter what, and it's going to cut its losses and send me to Roy.

It's worth a shot. And sitting here isn't going to accomplish anything other than give Maggie and Roy time to find each other.

Is that why it was so easy to just sit here? Did the loop let me take a break so Maggie and Roy could be drawn together somewhere? I wonder exactly how long I've been sitting on this curb, and it occurs to me that I've been suckered into walking all the way across town and waiting like an idiot so Maggie could wake up and go find Roy on her own.

She's probably on her way to him already. But at least if they're on a course to meet up, I know how to find them. The loop will bring me there.

As I push off from the curb, a searing pain in my chest

nearly doubles me over, and I drop to my knees, breathless. But the will of Fate drags me back to my feet and pushes me up. My chest burns and my breath is heavy, but I put my left foot in front of my right and start trudging across the parking lot toward the main road.

The farther I walk, the harder it is to breathe. My pace slows, and my feet drag across the pavement. My body feels like it weighs twice what it should. I cough and taste blood in my mouth.

I keep to the darkest parts of the street, drawing as little attention as possible. Fate steers me down alleys and side streets, keeping me out of the light. I must look like hell, limping along, bruised and spitting out blood every ten steps.

Still, I feel myself moving in a virtually straight line to my destination—cutting across vacant lots, crawling under parked tractor-trailers, and squeezing through barely open gates. The pull is too strong for me to take an easier path and stick to the sidewalks.

I slosh through murky puddles behind a Chinese restaurant and turn down a brick-walled alley, the only light coming from a neon sign two floors above. Fate pulls me onward as though she has me by the hand.

I arrive at a chain-link fence that stretches the width of the alley, with no way around or under. There is a Dumpster to one side, and I squirm up on top of it to get onto the fence, but there's still a few feet left to climb. My chest is burning and I'm gasping for breath as I push the toes of my sneakers into the chain-link and pull myself up, arms shaking from the weight of my body, my vision blurred from the pain.

At the top, I slide my leg over the side and half climb, half fall to the pavement below. I land on my knees and slump forward, coughing violently until blood has spattered onto the wet concrete inches from my nose.

I'm aware of the ache and burn from hitting the ground, but push it from my mind and lurch upright, marching like a machine toward Maggie. She's not far from here—less than a mile. I can feel it.

What if I'm too late? What if Roy already found her in the motel?

How would I know if something happened to her? I feel like I would just know it, sort of ESP-ish, maybe. I guess I'd probably be released from the loop, and I would *definitely* feel that.

Out of the loop I'd grow up. Grow old. Get married, even, though I can't imagine anyone but Maggie being with me forever.

But really I just want a little more *now*, more moments like when we made sandwiches at the Mission and danced together in the fog. I want to learn everything about her and hold her hand a little longer.

The loop has bonded us, stitched us together like Peter Pan and his shadow. Life without Maggie is beyond my imagination, unthinkable, like trying to imagine nothingness.

If I can't save her, I'm not sure I want to be saved, either.

twenty-eight

THE LIGHTS OF THE SHOPPING PLAZA glow like an airport runway, and despite the burning pain in my chest, I rush toward it at top speed. I can feel him there; I know Roy is out there somewhere, and an aching body and lungful of blood isn't going to keep me from getting to him. It occurs to me that Maggie has probably awakened by now and might be out looking for me.

Or maybe she's looking for Roy, too.

The thought has me refocused, and I power through the pain and gain some ground quickly, only to get careless and stumble over a crack in the pavement, falling hard and fast into the dark between cars. My hands burn as I push myself up, and in the amber glow from the parking lot lights I can see shards of glass buried deep in my palms. Green glass. A Heineken bottle, maybe?

I shake my hand, and most of the glass comes out on its own. But there are still a few pieces in there that I'll have to pull out. I'm not normally squeamish, but this turns my stomach.

I decide to go for the biggest piece first, a big triangle of sparkling green that is lodged in the center of my palm, right across a crease in the skin that, now that I think about it, might be my lifeline. Or so an old woman in Jackson Square once told me.

So ironic, and *totally* predictable.

I give the chunk of glass a hard pull, and it slides out—a lot bigger than I had thought it would be. Blood flows out of the wound and forms a puddle in my palm. I'm not sure how the glass didn't go clear through to the other side and out the back of my hand.

But as bad as it seems, I'm numb to it. I toss the glass to the asphalt and pull out the smaller pieces, and when I'm done, I've left a little collection of bloody green shards under a parking lot lamppost.

I wipe my bloody hands on my shirt and stagger on.

As I approach the entrance to Walgreens, the doors slide open for me: *Come on in, Ben,* they say.

I trudge through the doors, past the shoulder-high sensors that beep when you've stolen something, down the aisle with nail polish, and straight toward the rear of the store. At this time of night there are only a few shoppers in the aisles, but they freeze and stare as I pass. There's blood on my shirt, my chin, dripping from my hands. . . . I'm clutching my chest and wheezing with every step.

It occurs to me that I might look like a zombie.

Past the display of reading glasses, past the pharmacy in the back, and through the employees-only door under the giant domed antishoplifting mirror. Through the break room, past the clock with its rack of time cards, into the stockroom.

The pull is so strong at this point that I bet I could fall flat on my back and the loop would drag me to Maggie. I'm not conscious of moving my feet and legs. They just keep marching on their own, while the rest of my body sways limply, as though it's only along for the ride.

At the end of the stockroom is a gray metal door, and I turn the knob with my bloody left hand while putting my weight into it with my shoulder. It swings open and I spill outside into the parking lot.

It takes a moment for my eyes to adjust to the darkness, and when they do, I see one overhead lamp buzzing dimly.

Two figures stand in the circle of light below.

One is Maggie.

The other is Roy.

twenty-nine

MAGGIE'S ARMS HANG LIMPLY at her sides, her shoulders slumped forward. She stands pigeon-toed and barely lifts her head when I come through the door. Her eyes rise slowly to meet mine, tears on her cheeks, and she mouths two words:

I'm sorry.

Roy turns to me. "So sweet, you kids. I don't know how the two of you managed to keep yourselves out of my sight for so long this time."

He steps from behind Maggie, and I see a small black revolver in his hand. "But what's important, *kids,* is that you're both here now." A mask of mock concern sweeps across his face. "And, might I add . . . you two look like *crap.*"

It's true. We look like walking corpses. I'm spitting blood, and new bruises are still blooming on both Maggie and me. Roy should look pretty bad too, but he seems fine. Not a scratch on him—certainly not a bullet in his chest.

A loud bang splits the darkness, and Maggie and I jump. Roy only laughs—the door I'd come through has slammed shut behind me. I must have let it out of my grasp without realizing. My heart is racing.

Maggie's eyes meet mine, and she speaks very slowly, very clearly. "Ben, open the door."

I understand her words but can't make sense of them. I shake my head in confusion, and she says it again. "Ben. Open the door. The one behind you."

I reach behind me and find the knob without taking my eyes off of Roy. I twist and open it slowly, feeling the air-conditioned air pour out of the stockroom.

"Push the button in. On the knob." She's giving me instructions in this straight voice. I sense urgency, but she's trying to sound calm and make sure I understand. Roy hears it, too, but doesn't seem to get what she's up to.

Honestly, neither do I.

I push the center button in until I feel it click. I nod to Maggie, and she nods back, suddenly serious and alert. Her hands are clenched, and she raises one fist in front of her as though she's going to show off her bicep—then swings it down by her side and drives it straight into Roy's crotch.

Roy exhales with an *Oof!* and doubles over.

"GO!" Maggie yells, and before I can move, she's shoving me through the door.

She pulls the door closed behind us a split second before I hear Roy pounce on it, yanking at the knob on the other side. Maggie spins away, and a white envelope drops to the floor. I know right away it's the money from the OTB. I scoop it up and hand it to her.

"This way," she says, and grabs a fistful of my shirt, pulling me across the stockroom and around a shelf loaded with cases of soda. We crouch behind boxes of laundry detergent.

"This is it, Ben." Maggie's eyes are wide, pupils big and black like puddles of ink. The big bruise around her eye has grown dark, more black than purple. "This is when it happens." Her gaze bores into me. "We can hide, or we can fight."

I look around at the mountain of toilet paper, the stacks of cardboard boxes full of shampoo and cigarettes. "Fight? With what? Should we throw combs at him? You have plans for a tampon cannon or something?" I kick a rusty bolt across the floor. "We're screwed, Maggie."

Her face softens, dread fading into grief. She sighs, and her whole body deflates. "Yeah, we are."

She's still clenching my arm, stopping the blood from flowing to my hand—but I don't say a word. Maybe I make her feel better just by being there, even if I'm only something to be squeezed.

"Maggie?"

"Mmm."

"I'm sixteen years old. I don't want to die in a Walgreens."

She smiles, sad and sweet. "It won't be the first time, Ben. And hey"—she lets go of my arm and takes my hand—"maybe this is the one. Maybe we get it right this time around."

"Maybe." But I don't believe it.

She gives me a squeeze. I can't remember this moment clearly, but I know that there are only seconds left before Roy comes in and it's over.

Now or never, Romeo.

Maggie turns her face toward mine, and before I can chicken out or she can protest, I kiss her.

It's not a great kiss. It's fast and tentative. But it lands on her lips and she doesn't fight it.

In fact, she puts an arm around my neck and pulls me in for another. A much better one, too—longer.

This kiss is new. I know it.

For this moment, these few seconds, we are out of the loop. We're making a new history. And every cell in my body is praying that we're giving ourselves enough of an edge to bust out of the cycle and live to kiss again. And again and again.

Prayers are not enough.

The squeal of a rusty hinge splits the silence of the stockroom, and Maggie's eyes widen, panic spreading from her face to mine. "Here we go," she says, her voice unsteady.

She stuffs the envelope into the waist of her jeans and drops to her knees. Reaching under a crate topped with cases of bottled water, she emerges with a two-by-four that has three rusty nails sticking out of one end. Though it's only a few feet long, it makes for one gruesome weapon.

Maggie hands it to me, then reaches under a nearby shelf, coming up with a long steel hook—the kind used by warehouse workers to drag heavy pallets around.

I turn to slip behind a low shelf, and Maggie grabs my arm. "Not there," she says. "You get shot in the face there."

I shudder and find us a spot behind cases of air freshener. Crouching low, I realize that my breathing is heavy, and I try to muffle it with my hand. Every little movement, every heartbeat sounds a hundred times louder now, and I'm afraid that all the noise will give us away.

I try to slow my breathing. I try to calm my heart, but it just beats louder and faster.

And in walks Roy.

I hear him before I see him, his shoes echoing across the concrete floor. I feel cold all over, my skin turning clammy and my fingers trembling. He stops within spitting distance. His voice is deep, reverberant in the expansive stockroom. "You know it's over, you little bastards."

His shoe makes a soft *shhh* as it pivots on the cement; he turns toward us, homing in.

Before I can stop her, Maggie springs, swinging the hook at his chest. She misses by inches as he takes a neat step back, watching as Maggie falls to the floor. One quick jog forward, and his shoe is on her neck. He fakes a yawn, nodding in my direction. "Your turn, junior."

I rise slowly, legs weak, everything numb. He points to my board with its twisted nails. "Drop your little club, Benjamin."

I nod, but before letting the two-by-four slip from my hand, I twist my whole body, wind it up like a corkscrew, and swing with everything I have.

Roy barely has time to react as one of the nails tears through his cheek and draws blood.

Then, in one smooth movement, his right hand sweeps forward and I see the gun. Small, black—almost anticlimactic. The muzzle flashes bright white, and the sound of the shot rebounds off every surface in the stockroom.

My chest is on fire. I land hard on the concrete, head turned toward Maggie. Her eyes are filled with terror as Roy lifts his shoe from her neck, bending to take the envelope of cash from her jeans.

She pulls in a deep breath and whispers, "I love you," a moment before he presses the muzzle to her temple and fires a second time.

I know it's too late and she's already gone, but I manage to get it out before I'm gone with her. "I love you, too."

That's the last thing I say. My right arm grows warm as my own blood pools around it—everything else feels cold. I suck in one last stuttering breath before it all turns to black.

And I die.

thirty

I CAME INTO THE WORLD in the middle of the night at Tulane Hospital in New Orleans, Louisiana. My mother always told me the delivery was a breeze, though I can't imagine delivering a nine-pound baby girl being easy. My early childhood was surprisingly average. I had friends and did well in school, all signs pointing to normal. Dad gave me a skateboard for my sixth birthday, and it was my favorite thing in the world. Sometimes, on those rare cool days at the end of summer, we'd go to Audubon Park, and I'd ride it on the bike paths.

But by seventh grade, it was clear that "normal" was not in the cards. In a few short years I'd had four rounds of déjà vu—usually for a couple of days at a time—and I couldn't manage to cover up my knack for knowing what came next.

During those spells I'd blurt out the answer to a question I couldn't possibly know, or comment on how awful the lunch was that we hadn't even been served yet. I was labeled a psychic, a witch. Of course, being anything but average in seventh grade sucked, but being an all-out freak was hell. All I wanted was to fit in—or to become the Invisible Girl, whichever was easier. Probably the latter.

The first time it happened, I had no idea what was going on. It didn't occur to me that I might have already *lived* through the same couple of days over and over. I just knew that all at once everything was unsettlingly familiar—and I couldn't understand why.

That first loop spanned half of a day, give or take. It began one morning during the summer after sixth grade, when Mom and I were in the supermarket. I remember suddenly feeling . . . *different*. It was sort of a detached sensation. Of course at the time, I didn't yet understand that I was caught in a loop that was putting me through the paces for probably the thousandth time.

Dad had moved to Baton Rouge less than a year before, and Mom and I were finally getting back to being near each other without our conversations always ending in an argument. It was very intense after Dad moved away—Mom and I needed each other desperately, but we sort of blamed each other, too. For a while we'd scream at one another before leaving for school or work with the kind of regularity most people reserve for daily rituals like morning coffee or getting the mail.

It had started as a good day—we were both in an excellent mood, making jokes, laughing at a malformed potato that looked way too much like my friend Ashley's mom. Ironically, I remember wishing I could bookmark that morning and be able to come back to it and live it over again.

It came on like a floodlight. I went around a corner in the frozen foods section and all of a sudden the déjà vu was overwhelming, like everything around me was part of a show I'd already seen. I didn't quite have it *memorized,* but the show held few surprises.

Things kept coming to me in flashes: I knew the groceries would come to ninety-seven dollars and fifty-eight cents at the checkout. I knew Mom would stop short when she backed out of our parking space because some old lady came out of nowhere and was suddenly behind us on one of those little motorized scooters. I knew the *Picayune* would be all over our yard when we got home because the Fredericksons' dog got loose and liked to steal newspapers off porches and make confetti out of them.

And I must have embarrassed myself at *some* point during a turn in that loop, because in certain situations I instinctively knew to keep it to myself when I recognized something specific. Like in line at the supermarket, before the total came up on the register, I wanted to yell out "NINETY-SEVEN DOLLARS AND FIFTY-EIGHT CENTS," but something stronger, a little voice of reason in my head, told me to keep my trap shut.

That little voice inside wasn't *always* there, though. Sometimes, in later loops, I would blurt out something that there was no way I could know, and everyone around me would freeze. Eyes would widen and mouths would go slack, then fingers would point, the classroom erupting in whispers.

And as suddenly as the déjà vu had begun, it ended. Back to normal. Well—not exactly *normal.* I had humiliated myself and the damage was done. My classmates never looked at me the same way again—their faces always betrayed their suspicion, or mockery—sometimes, even a little fear.

That was the birth of the rumors. The psychic. The witch.

Once when I was thirteen, the whole class went on a field trip to the New Orleans Museum of Art. I sat in the middle of the bus—the popular kids sat in the back, the teachers sat in the front, and those who preferred to be overlooked and ignored sat in the middle. I had my earbuds in and stared out the window as we rolled along in the slow lane on highway 610.

All day I'd known something bad was coming. I was in a loop that probably started in the middle of the night, because it was there when I woke up. And as soon as I rolled over and opened my eyes, I had a feeling of dread: I *knew* there was something terrible in store. That feeling hung over me through breakfast, through the ride to school, and it was still with me as I stared through the window on the bus to the museum.

When it happened, it happened fast. And as suddenly as

I knew what was going to happen, I knew I was powerless to prevent it. Bending Fate was a concept I wouldn't even attempt until my next loop; this time, for all I knew I was just along for the ride.

Mike Carter was sitting in the row in front of me, and he was kneeling on his seat, trying to slide the window closed. It was only open a couple inches, I don't know what the big deal was—but he was really putting some muscle into it, leaning in with his whole body.

The littlest finger on his left hand was wrapped around the metal edge of the window. I saw it coming a mile away.

I managed to stand and leaned over and said, *Mike, get your finger out of the window*. He didn't hear me. And just as he gave it one last, giant effort, the bus stopped short. The tires gave a loud *chirp*, and everyone pitched forward into the back of someone else's seat.

The window slammed shut. Mike's pinkie finger dropped to the pavement below. Everyone near us screamed except for him—he just stared at his hand, watching all the blood roll out. It slithered down over his wrist and disappeared into the sleeve of his hoodie.

I jumped from my seat and yanked off my jacket, wrapping it around his hand. I suppose I knew I should have used something sterile, but it's not like I had a pharmacy full of options. I held the balled-up jacket there while we waited for an ambulance to come.

A few girls heard me try to warn Mike, and they told their friends about it. And those friends told theirs. I didn't have any friends, so I didn't bother trying to tell anyone anything.

Damage done.

I grew my hair long enough to cover my face—not much of an insulating layer, I know, but I liked being able to hide behind something, even if it was just bangs. I wore lots of black; it just seemed the appropriate choice at the time. Not a legit goth girl, you know, just dark, sending out that "don't bother talking to me because I'm only going to stare back at you" vibe that works so well at keeping everyone at a distance. And my iPod was always in my pocket, with the earbuds permanently jammed in my head, even if I didn't have any music on. If anyone spoke, I could pretend not to hear.

I knew everyone stared and talked about me, but I also knew there was nothing I could do about it. It was all part of the cycle—the whispering, the iPod, the freak factor.

During my fourth episode of déjà vu, a twenty-hour borefest during a road trip to Chicago, I had started to piece it together. I spent that whole loop in the car, staring out the window and listening to music. Nothing but time to kill.

The boredom of the car ride let me focus on tuning in to that feeling of knowing what color car was going to pass us next—or occasionally, what the license plate might read. And at some point on that drive I began to tinker with the idea that maybe I wasn't seeing the *future*, so much as I was seeing the *present again*. Bizarre as that idea was, it was no crazier than thinking I was a psychic, or a clairvoyant. And with that thought came a strong feeling that I was on to something.

That idea felt comfortable. It felt right.

After all, living your life over again isn't such a novel concept—doesn't Hinduism subscribe to something like that? Living an endless cycle of birth and death?

It's probably not quite the same thing.

But having a theory, no matter how flimsy, as to what was happening to me was comforting. Better to believe in some ridiculous cosmic time warp than the possibility I was going completely insane, right?

Right.

Late one Saturday afternoon at the end of my sophomore year, I took the bus to the mall. It was hot, even for June, and I looked forward to the air-conditioning almost as much as I looked forward to seeing Ben.

I must have checked my hair a dozen times in the bus window.

I got off the bus at the usual time, strolled through the mall entrance in the usual way, grabbed a pretzel at the place next to Sunglass Hut the same way I had a million times before. It was like watching the most boring movie *ever*—over and over and over. Time for the bald guy to pass by sipping an iced coffee . . . cue the bald guy . . . ready, and—

Action!

thirty-one

I STAND AT THE RAILING on the second floor, overlooking the food court and the escalator. I watch Ben turn the corner and walk my way, my heart already beating fast from the anticipation of the moment. I try to visualize how I *want* it to go, not the way it has always *gone*—and make my way to the escalator.

I see him step on at the bottom. I wait.

He's halfway up. I'm still waiting. And waiting.

A little nauseated.

I stand out of sight behind a woman with a stroller, move my backpack from one shoulder to the other, palms sweating. Waiting. Waiting.

I've been preparing for this moment for weeks, trying to train my body to fight back against the loop and let me do my own thing at this very moment. Every little push the loop gave me, I pushed back. Hard. Every time I bent Fate, I imagined myself here at the escalator, so when the time came I could do this one trick, this simple little thing to put a smile on his face and let Ben know I haven't forgotten him.

I focus on the tiles beneath my feet and name the states under my breath.

Ben steps off at the top, looks left, then right. I focus every molecule of my being into controlling my actions, and take two steps into view. Ben freezes when he sees me, and then looks down, puzzled, at the cup of iced tea in his hand.

"Aren't I supposed to be wearing this tea on my shirt by now?"

"My gift to you," I say.

I can't help grinning like an idiot, pleased with myself at my change in the loop. It was just a little thing, but I can tell he's impressed.

Ben smiles the sweetest smile I've ever seen, and drops the still-full cup in the trash. "You look beautiful," he says.

We rocket around a corner, heading for Seventeenth Street, and right on schedule we crash into a man in a yellow T-shirt and jeans. All three of us end up on the ground. Ben gets to his feet and takes a step toward me, his hand out to help me up, but freezes when he sees who we smacked into.

While he's collecting himself, I make my leap for the gun that clatters to the sidewalk, snatching it just in the nick of time. Ben snaps out of his daze and shouts Roy's name, buying me just the fraction of a second I need to get my hands around it and level it at Roy's chest.

Roy puts his hands up, kneeling, his face warped into a greasy smile. "Well . . . this is new, sweetheart."

"Shut up." I give the gun a flick, and Roy flinches. It feels good. "I could kill you right now. And I'm thinking maybe I should. Shouldn't I, Benjamin?"

I look over at Ben. "Whatever you think is best," he says.

Lame.

Roy's smile widens, his eyes shining. "You won't kill me. That's not how it goes. You can't change the big picture, Maggie."

He is standing now, inching closer. "You can mess around with the details now and then, sure. Like Ben's little ad-lib here. But you can't change the master plan."

I let the scene run mostly on autopilot. I know it by heart. But while my limbs are moving and my mouth is speaking, my brain is scrambling to solve something that bothered me last time through the cycle, but I hadn't been able to put my finger on it.

Then I see it: just a hint of black peeking out through the neck of his shirt.

A bulletproof vest.

That sly rat—I wonder how many cycles ago he started wearing it. It certainly explains his lack of a gunshot wound the last time around. And in a weird way, it makes sense: For my plan to work, we need to follow the script and Roy needs to keep breathing.

For now.

I squeeze the gun tight in my fist and fire, plugging Roy dead center, the recoil of the gun in my hand startling me as much as the impact of the bullet must have startled *him*. He reels back and falls to the pavement, clutching his chest.

And we run.

thirty-two

WHAT AN ASS. I can't believe Ben left me here, my hands tied behind me, strapped to the bus station bench with his belt.

Right here in the middle of the room, everyone and their uncle walking by, and I'm tied up like Houdini. At least he had the decency to cover my hands with a magazine so nobody sees that I'm bound up like some kind of kidnapping victim.

But the fact that I'm fighting back tears doesn't make me any less conspicuous.

I'm already tugging at the leather around my wrists as the bus pulls away, but it's a good ten minutes before I can slip my pinkie into the buckle and pull a loop through to free myself. At this point, I don't know what to do—it's like when we broke free of the cycle and went into the Quarter to see Steve. Not having the feeling of being caught in a track that steers your every move is totally disorienting. I just sit for a bit, trying to decide what to do next.

It's no use—I feel lost. Not only can I not see what's going to come next, I don't even have Ben with me to help think things through. He isn't the smartest kid I know, but when it comes down to it, he can handle himself. And I'd be lying if I said I didn't need him just to help me get through each minute of our loop. Now that he's gone, I can feel how much of my strength was actually drawn from his. Or maybe our strength came from simply being together; all I know is that without him I feel weak, inside and out.

So this is being in love.

He always gets so nervous when we don't have anything to talk about. I can see his brain spinning in his head, trying to come up with something clever to say, something to break the silence.

It's those silent times when I think about kissing him, just going for it whether he's ready or not. I think about kissing him a lot, actually. I try not to; I try to keep my head in the game and worry about our survival. But I can't help it.

I talk the lady at the ticket window into swapping my Shreveport boarding pass for one to Biloxi. She slips the new ticket under the glass, and I stuff it in my back pocket.

The three o'clock bus sits idling, waiting, exhaling that diesel haze in the air. It's a new bus—I can smell the vinyl seats and rubber flooring in the aisle as I walk on. I slump into a window seat.

I don't know how long I sleep. The rumble of the big engine and the hum of the highway knock me out like anesthesia after a few minutes. I don't even remember what I dream about.

But I do know that what wakes me up is the sudden quiet.

I sit up and peer through the tinted windows, seeing that we're stopped at a kind of rest area, a little parking lot just off the highway, lined with tractor-trailers and campers. The bus door is open and the driver's seat is empty.

I should have known this would happen. Fate has a knack for getting what she wants.

We sit there forever, with a mechanic banging around outside and the driver assuring us that we'll be on our way soon enough.

The air-conditioning isn't running, and pretty soon the bus starts to really heat up. The old ladies up front are the first to start complaining, but eventually it's everybody. Well, everybody except me—I'm actually grateful to stay put. It occurs to me that I can't be going to Shreveport if I'm totally stationary. Maybe my luck is changing.

Of course, nothing truly good lasts for very long, and the engine fires up, to the cheers of the ladies up front. We idle for a few more minutes, the mechanic pointing to the engine with a greasy finger and explaining the issue to the driver, who nods impatiently and clearly just wants to get back on the road.

He climbs the steps and closes the door behind him, keeping the noise of the highway out and the air-conditioning in. "Folks, we have a little issue with the bus. We're up and running for now, enough to get us to Slidell, but those of you continuing on to Gulfport and Biloxi will have to be put on another bus, and it may be some time before we have one ready for you."

Complaints come flying from every seat but mine. I'm not really sure how I feel about it. My paranoid side is pretty well convinced that this is the beginning of Fate's plan to push me west. But I won't know for sure until I see where it leads.

I sink down into my seat and watch the guardrail slither by, rising and falling like a wave on the ocean.

In Slidell, we all wander around the station while we wait for the replacement bus to arrive from, well, wherever it is. We're given vouchers for a free drink from the little snack bar, and I get an iced coffee.

An hour later, I come out of the restroom and see one of my bus mates boarding a Greyhound. I figure that I've missed the announcement about the bus being ready to depart, so I follow, taking a seat in the back.

Looking around, I don't recognize any of the faces from the previous bus.

Hmm. Suddenly concerned.

I turn to the man sitting across the aisle. "Were you on the bus from New Orleans, the one that broke down?"

"Sure was. Bunch of bull, if you ask me."

I breathe a sigh of relief. "Yeah, I though so, too. Making us wait in that heat and everything."

It's funny how I've only been apart from my iPod for a day, yet it seems like years since I've had it in my pocket. Bus rides are *made* for listening to music and dozing off. I'm anticipating a long, dull ride, but the bus pulls away from the station, and before I know it I've drifted off again, the hum of the highway singing me to sleep.

thirty-three

"HEY, WAKE UP, KID. We're in Baton Rouge. Are you getting off here?"

I push the hair out of my face and see the man I talked to when I first got on the bus. "No, I'm going to Biloxi, but thanks for—"

I freeze. "You said we're in Baton Rouge?"

The man nods. "I sure did."

"But that's . . . that's the wrong way. That's toward Shreveport. I thought you said you were on the Biloxi bus before."

"I *was.* While we were waiting for the next bus, I got a call from my nephew up in Alexandria. His wife is real sick. I figured I'd swap my ticket and pop in to see them."

The man's eyes narrow, the wrinkles around them deepening and multiplying, his big gray eyebrows dropping. "You sure look worried. You didn't get on the wrong bus, did you?"

I try to get up from my seat, but Fate's hand holds me firm. She wants me with Ben so bad that she put me onto the first bus straight to him. I can't fight it, and I sink back into my seat. This is a different pull than when the two of us are fighting to break out of the loop—this is Fate pulling me back to Ben, and there's no fighting it this time. We're supposed to be together, and at the moment, Fate's word seems to be final.

"No," I sigh. "I'm on the right bus."

After fifteen minutes of sitting, the bus pulls out and rolls back onto the highway. This time, though, I don't fall asleep.

I've always known Fate is strong, and I've respected her power of keeping everything on track, but I hadn't realized that she was *creative.* I figured that once I broke free of the cycle and went on my own, she'd lose her hold over me. But here I am, on a bus to Shreveport.

This, of course, makes me wonder what other things she's capable of.

The next stop is Alexandria, about a hundred miles or so south of Shreveport. I'm sleepy again from the motion of the bus and the excitement of the day, and part of me wants nothing more than to just give up and let myself be carried off to Shreveport. I'd be killed by nightfall, but then in a sense be born again, and maybe I'd try harder to change my luck next time.

Quite tempting in its simplicity.

But I know. I know this shot is our best one, maybe our only one. Ben and I have thrown the cycle so far out of whack that it seems like now or never. If we can't get away from it this time, I doubt we ever can.

I'm exhausted—I know we *both* are—but there's a feeling I have that tells me to keep pushing forward, to keep fighting. For all of the setbacks and obstacles thrown our way, we have a kind of momentum going for us that I don't think we can afford to waste. What if the next time through the loop, Fate doesn't go so easy on us and pushes harder to get us to Shreveport? As many times as I've been through this, I still don't really know how it works. I doubt anyone does.

This time, our chance of breaking out is better than it's ever been, and maybe better than it ever will be.

No giving in today.

One thing I've noticed in the last two days is that the more we change the cycle, the easier it becomes to bend Fate. That gives me some hope of getting off the bus at the stop in Alexandria before it continues on to Shreveport. I try to visualize rising from my seat and walking down the aisle, jogging down the steps and hopping off the bus when it arrives at the next station.

"You seem nervous." It's the man across the aisle, the one whose nephew had the sick wife.

"I am." It feels odd admitting it, but the man looks very kind, and I'm too tired to make up anything better than the truth.

"First time traveling by yourself?"

"No. First time going to Alexandria, though."

The man smiles. "Oh, it's a decent town. You'll like it well enough, I guess. Not much to see, really. You have friends there?"

I shake my head.

"Oh. Family, then?"

I shake my head again.

"Well. Everybody's got their reason for hitting the road, I suppose."

He pulls his sleeve back and eyes his watch. "We ought to be getting in any minute now. Do you know where you're going from here?"

"Not really, no." He seems concerned, and I feel bad. "But I'll be fine, really. Don't have to worry."

"Oh, I'm sure you'll do all right. Do you have money at least?" He reaches into his coat pocket.

I just have a little change. "Not much, no."

"Well, look—" He opens his wallet. "It's not a lot, but at my age you learn to make do with what the government sends you. Which is, well, not a lot. Take this. I won't miss it, I promise."

He holds a twenty in his fingers and reaches across the aisle. "Really, I'd just spend it on beer anyhow." He laughs.

"No, I couldn't. I mean—" But I don't know how to finish. I need the money. I take the bill and smile. "Thank you; you're very kind."

"Aw, it's nothing. Like I said, I'd just waste it anyway. Now look at that, here we are already."

The bus slows and eases into the station, the lights of the depot an oasis in the surrounding darkness.

"Thank you," I say again.

The old man meets his nephew and they drive off in a station wagon. I stand by the street and weigh my options: left or right.

Both directions look pretty much the same. To the left is an uninteresting line of brightly lit sidewalks and darkened storefronts. To the right is more of the same, but perhaps better odds of finding a place to eat.

I can feel it again, the gentle push of Fate guiding my steps. I don't bother to fight.

I walk for almost a quarter of a mile before I come to a diner. With every step I take, I feel the pull growing stronger. Ben and I are magnets, and I can picture myself being lifted from the ground and flying through the diner's glass doors when I cross some invisible threshold.

I can see through the windows that it's busy inside, but I go in anyway. Somehow I know there will be a table for me.

thirty-four

No matter how many times I ride this loop, I know I will never get over how bad the enchiladas in the MREs taste. Maybe it isn't so much about the taste as it is the consistency of the tortilla, or whatever tortilla-substitute the military came up with. At least the crackers and peanut butter are edible.

"You know, it's pretty amazing," I say. "All the trips through the loop we've made, you and I have never been a day older than we are right now. That's big. We've never been this old before."

Ben nods slowly. "We should celebrate."

"Whatcha have in mind, Romeo?"

• • •

It's like a dream. I know from the outside it must look *tacky,* a boy and a girl slow dancing in the headlights like this. It's like something out of a bad horror movie: The boy pretends to run out of gas on an empty country road. The girl knows what he's up to but doesn't care because she's kind of hoping *tonight's the night,* but they don't get any further than a slow dance because the werewolf or horde of zombies or crazy guy with hooks for hands comes out of the woods and tears them to shreds.

It does have that vibe. But I don't care. Being here with Benjamin, with him holding me, my hands locked together behind his back, anchoring him close to me—it's the perfect moment. The music, the fog, everything is just the way it should be, and I don't care if it's been the stupidest scene in a thousand awful movies. I feel safe here, and this is all I could ever want.

And besides, there's nothing that could creep out of those woods that's half as scary as knowing what's in store for us this time tomorrow.

"You're a good dancer," I tell him.

"Because I haven't fallen down yet?"

"Because right now I don't want to be anywhere else."

We sit in the car, seats back, watching the sky through the windshield. There's a lot that I want to say to Ben, but I just don't have the strength to push against Fate and come up with something new.

"I really enjoyed not getting murdered with you tonight, Ben."

"I enjoyed not getting murdered with you, too," he says.

I let my hand drift toward his, my fingers curled around his, just soaking in the moment.

"Ben?"

"Yeah?" His voice is higher pitched than usual. I think it's because I'm touching him.

"If it doesn't work out for us, you know, I've had way more fun this trip through the loop than I've ever had before. It was really different this time, and I just wanted to say that if we die tonight, or tomorrow, I can't wait to meet you again on the escalator."

"Sure," he says. "Me too." He takes a breath as though he's about to say something, but nothing comes. It's okay, though. This moment is perfect.

I feel my hand in his and close my eyes, hoping to drift off soon so I don't lie awake waiting for the crash to come.

thirty-five

I CAN'T BELIEVE HE LEFT ME *AGAIN*.

One minute it's morning and he's helping me through the door, sitting me on the bed in the motel, pulling my shoes off. Next thing I know, I wake up alone.

It seems like no time has passed at all when I open my eyes, yet it's already getting dark out. I must have slept, what—eight, nine hours? I crawl out of bed and see that Ben has taken off. At least he didn't strap me to a bus station bench this time.

He thinks he's saving me. He thinks he'll take on Roy by himself and do whatever manly hero crap boys daydream about.

He's insane. If he's still alive, that is.

I check myself over in the bathroom mirror. I have much

better light than I did in the hospital, and I'm shocked at how beat-up I look. The black eye is a disturbing dark purple. I knew it must be a pretty serious bruise, because my whole face hurts when I squint or try to smile; but it still looks much worse than I had expected.

If I had my backpack I could paint myself up with concealer. *A lot* of concealer.

My shoulder is sore and it hurts to move my right arm. My bottom lip is swollen, and there's a cut on it that still bleeds a little. Farther down, my hip aches and has stiffened up. Makes me walk like an old lady. I find another bruise there, right on my pelvis, and I'm thinking that's where I got hit the hardest. It's too sore to touch.

The rest of me feels like—well, it feels like I was hit by a truck.

At first I panic because I'm not sure how to find Ben. I know I was in this situation the last time through, but it's hazy—too hazy to remember what comes next. I can't let him face Roy alone, and I have no idea where to begin looking for him. Not that I'd be much help in a fight in the shape I'm in, but I can't let him get himself killed trying to be a gentleman.

Then I realize how ridiculously easy finding Ben will be. All I need to do is relax and the loop will lead me to him.

And to Roy.

I pull my sneakers on and check the mirror again— Yup, I still look like hell. With no makeup around, the best I can do is keep my hair down over that eye and try not to limp too badly. No money in my pocket, nothing in the motel room worth taking. Good luck, Maggie.

I try to clear my mind, to feel like an empty bottle floating on the ocean. I tell myself I'll wash up where Fate wants me, and until then I'm just riding the current.

I sit on the edge of the bed and close my eyes, my breath coming slowly and evenly. I picture a vast, calm sea, and I'm floating on my back in the middle of it. My body is a compass needle, supersensitive to the magnetic pull of the loop.

I stand. My eyes are still closed, and I take three steps forward. Another three steps and I extend my hand, wrapping my fingers around the doorknob. I don't need to see it; Fate puts my hand right where it needs to be.

I open my eyes and I'm in the current, tuned in to the feel of Fate's hand on my back, guiding me toward Ben.

The current takes me out the door and into the dark, six blocks down and left at the liquor store. Seven more blocks, past a used-car place, a coffee shop, a Laundromat. A pizza place. A dry cleaner.

I come to a bench and sit down. An older woman at the end of the bench offers a polite smile, but I can tell she's seen my black eye and my crooked walk and thinks I'm some crackhead runaway who will make a grab for her purse the second she looks away. So she keeps her eye on me.

Ten minutes pass. A bus comes, and I get up to board, but realize that I don't have any money for the fare. The woman at the end of the bench clears her throat in that "Pardon me, I need your attention" sort of way.

"Miss—I think you dropped your fare." She points to the sidewalk at my feet.

I'm not at all surprised to find, trapped under the toe of my sneaker, three one-dollar bills. How about that—Fate even gave me a couple extra bucks in case I get thirsty. I scoop the money up and push one of the bills into the slot as I get on the bus.

Another eight or nine minutes pass, stops come and go, riders get off and new ones get on. The doors open in a pretty sketchy part of town, on a corner near a place that offers "Payday advances, check cashing, and bail bonds." I silently pray that Fate knows what she's doing as I rise from my seat.

Off the bus. Walk three blocks, stop in front of a building with a sign for off-track betting.

I stand there for six minutes. It finally hits me that I know this place well. The windows, the cracks in the sidewalk, and the sound track of passing cars and distant voices play like a scene in a movie I've watched thousands of times before.

It seems that Fate has put things on pause for me, in a way. Ben and I have already lived a day longer in the loop than we ever have before, so you'd think all those events that happened last time through would have occurred and been over by now. But even though I'm a day later than usual, everything here is as I remember it from before.

An older man hobbles toward the door, a guy with a cane and a kind face. He's wearing a nice hat, one of those brown short-brimmed felt ones. He sees me and touches it, a quick gesture of Southern manners. He flashes a smile, and I smile back.

"Pardon me, sir," I say. "I'm in a little bit of a pinch, and I was wondering if you could do me a tiny favor."

"I've never denied a pretty girl in need if I could help it." The man's entire face wrinkles when he smiles. It's dark enough out on the sidewalk that I'm pretty sure most of my bruises don't show—but still, the smile fades and a look of concern crosses his face as he leans closer to me. "Looks like you been through the wringer, miss. If you don't mind my saying."

"I'm fine, really. I just need a little help." I hold my thumb and index finger an inch apart. "A little, *tiny* bit of help."

The old man nods, but glances at a neon Budweiser sign in a window across the street. "Oh, you don't want me to buy you liquor, do you?"

"Oh, no, it's not that. I have two dollars here, and well, I just have a funny feeling about the horse race at seven. You ever get one of those funny feelings?"

"Well, you know—I have," he says.

"Will you place a bet for me, then? Of course if I win, I'll give you a good cut of it." I offer my sweetest smile and even bat my eyelashes just to close the deal.

"I suppose it couldn't do any harm," he says. "I'll be right back."

He disappears inside only to reemerge a moment later with a pencil and a betting form. He slips the paper to me casually, and I mark off my bet.

"Trifecta?" the man says. "That must be some feeling you have. I knew a fella who hit the trifecta one time. Won almost fifty grand on a five-dollar bet."

Seven minutes later the old man leans through the doorway, his face pale and serious.

"Miss," he says, "I never believed in miracles before. But I do now."

He looks left and right as though checking for eavesdroppers. "I'll cash in your form in a minute. Meet me out back."

I walk along the side of the building to the rear of the OTB, where a single bulb over the back door illuminates the area. There is only a Dumpster and a car that was built long before I was born and probably hasn't run in at least a decade. It's on cinder blocks and filled with garbage. The whole place smells like a swamp.

The back door opens and the old man shuffles out, checking over his shoulder nervously. He leans close to me and whispers as he hands over the envelope.

"Twenty-nine thousand, four hundred and eighteen dollars, sixty-five cents. A lesser man would be ten blocks away with this money by now." He shakes his head. "Lord help me, I'd be lying to you if I said it didn't cross *my* mind once or twice when I cashed in that form."

"Oh, I wouldn't blame you," I say. I pull some money out and start counting. "Here. This is for your trouble." I hand him a stack of bills, ten thousand dollars.

"Miss"—the man's hand trembles as he takes the money—"thank you. I hope someday I'll see you again so I can repay your kindness."

I smile weakly, doing my best to fake it despite the pain in my body. "Actually, if it would make you feel better, there is one more thing you could do for me."

The old man nods eagerly, though I notice a trace of suspicion in his eyes. "Of course. Whatever I can do."

"Well . . . it's a little unusual, but I need you to make a call for me, in . . ." I pause, thinking through my next set of moves. "Twenty minutes?"

He arches his eyebrows. "A phone call? Well, shoot—it's the least I can do."

thirty-six

"GO!"

I give Ben a rough push through the door just as Roy comes charging after us, managing to slam it shut behind me not a split second too late. I pull Ben by the shirt across the stockroom floor.

Time to take charge. I push back against every natural inclination I have; every rut that Fate wants me to slip into, I fight my way out of.

I grab Ben by the hand and lead him to the far side of the room, pushing him past the usual spots where we've been killed before, and behind a pallet of floor cleaner. We crouch there, catching our breath.

"Maggie?"

"Mmm."

"I don't want to die in a Walgreens."

"I know, Ben. I don't either." I'm still holding his hand, and I give it a squeeze, searching my brain for something clever to say, when Ben beats me to it.

"I love you, Maggie."

I'm speechless. Ben takes my hand and pulls me close to him, then kisses me.

It's a good one. I wrap both arms around him and bury my face in his shoulder, wishing I could live here forever, right here, holding Benjamin.

"Maggie?"

My throat tightens, and little tears gather at the edges of my vision. For the first time since I woke up this morning, nothing hurts.

"I love you, too," I say.

I hear Roy before I see him, his footsteps clicking across the room. He has eased the door open just enough to slither through, and he walks straight to the spot where Ben and I have hidden countless times before. His back is to us, but his words ring out clearly.

"You know it's over, you little bastards."

We've found a new spot, a niche between stacks of paper towels at the far end of the stockroom, and through the gap we can see Roy play out his routine. His hand slips into his coat pocket and emerges with a gun—small, black—and he lets it hang coolly at his side.

It's a strange moment, seeing it play from this angle. I half expect to see myself spring from our hiding place in front of him, swinging my steel hook, then Roy taking that step back to dodge it and pinning me under his heel. Instead, only silence.

It's so quiet I can hear Ben breathing next to me. I can feel his pulse race where my hand is wrapped around his, and his skin has gone damp and cold like mine. The side effects of not letting the loop tell us what to do.

Roy stiffens, suddenly aware that things are not going as they should. He takes a hesitant step forward, peering over the cases of air freshener.

"Damn it!" he roars. "Where are you? Just make it easy on yourselves and come on out. You know you can't fight what's meant to be."

He begins a search, sticking his gun into every space under the shelves before tearing the boxes away to reveal another empty hiding spot. "Just let it happen," he says.

The hunt is systematic. Beginning at the end of the room where he'd expected to find us, he makes his way toward our side, exposing every potential bit of cover we could have squeezed into. Boxes fall, contents spill. Cans of coffee roll across the floor.

I become aware that I'm crushing Ben's hand in my own, but I doubt he feels it. His attention is glued to the gap between the boxes we're hiding behind, watching Roy storm his way toward us. Every second, Roy is one step closer to ending our lives and sending us back to the beginning. Completing our loop.

He is maybe twenty feet away. In seconds he'll be on us. I need more time.

More boxes fall, closer and closer. Bottles of shampoo scatter across the concrete. One of them rolls our way and comes to rest at my feet.

"I may not kill you fast this time. I may make you suffer for pissing me off like this." The stacks of cigarette cartons next to us bounce aside, Roy's foot kicking them away with far more force than necessary.

"Strike that. I'm *definitely* going to make you suffer." He moves directly in front of us.

The box that is inches from our faces is suddenly torn away. The blazing overhead lights flood our vision and obscure Roy's face. All I can make out are his shoes.

"Stand up, you little bitch," he says. His teeth are clenched through every word. "Your boyfriend, too. Slowly."

I rise, legs shaking. Ben stands, too, putting his arm around me and pulling me close. Roy raises the gun to my head.

"Wait," I shout.

Time. I need time. My gaze darts around the stockroom, reaching for anything to keep us breathing a little longer. A million thoughts flash through my head, things to say to gain a few seconds, things I should make a note of to do differently next time.

"Wait," I say again. "I need to know one thing."

Roy keeps the gun leveled at my forehead but tilts his head in curiosity, as though he's heard a strange noise. "And what's that?"

"What happens after this? After you kill us, what's next? Do you get away with it?" Icy sweat rolls down my cheek, over goose bumps and bruises, following the line of my jaw down to my chin. It waits for a moment before falling, and my senses are so hyped up right now I swear I can hear the drop hit the cement floor.

Roy's shoulders slacken, his expression softening. "Not sure. It's always hazy from this point on. Hell, maybe I die too—not that it matters. This is what I'm *here* for. This is my job, and that's all there is." His fingers tighten around the grip of the gun. "There is nothing else in the world that matters at all. Nothing."

He lowers the gun just a fraction, his eyes squinting as he works to put a thought together. It's like watching a shark with a Rubik's Cube: His brain isn't made for creating new ideas. His brain is only there to get him from A to B, to get the job done and that's all. I can see that clearly now that we are face-to-face.

"You know," he says, "I don't even know if I'll still exist. After I kill you two, I mean." He shrugs. "I could just . . . disappear. Like smoke."

Just then, immediately to our left, a metal door opens softly. Fluorescent lighting spills into the stockroom around the shadow of a figure standing in the doorway. Roy snaps back to the present, the gun held high, his eyes fixed on mine like a panther locked on to some lame, injured prey.

A man's voice: "Sir, I need you to lower your weapon, *now.*"

Roy keeps the gun aimed at my head.

The man in the doorway takes three steps closer, his own gun raised. "Sir, I need you to lower your weapon. *Now.*"

"This may sound funny to you," Roy says, "but I can't. It's not my choice. It's my destiny."

Roy's eyes narrow in anticipation of the explosion from the barrel, every muscle stiffening. His finger tenses on the trigger and he squeezes.

Boom.

thirty-seven

ROY LIES AT MY FEET, blood pooling quickly around my shoes. I can smell it, coppery and nauseating.

The police officer kicks the gun from Roy's limp hand and crouches, checking for a pulse. From the river of blood on the floor and the massive hole in the side of his head, I'm guessing there will be no sign of life, but I suppose procedure is procedure.

The cop checks anyway and looks up at Ben and me.

"You two okay? Are you hurt?"

We both shake our heads.

"How did you . . . Why did you come here?" Ben asks. "How did you know to come here?"

The officer stands and speaks into his radio, reporting the incident in numeric codes and short phrases that I'm sure are

English—I just don't understand them. My mind can't wrap around the reality of the situation:

Roy is dead and we are not.

The conversation on the radio takes priority over explaining the matter to us, but between phrases to the dispatcher, the cop explains how he came to be here.

"We received a call about half an hour ago, some guy at a bar down the road said he saw a man matching this description"—the officer gestures to the corpse on the floor—"abducting two youths from the sidewalk. The guy said he followed them a little ways and saw him bring you in here. The guy who phoned the tip in got spooked, I guess. We have a unit trying to locate him, but I think my report will be enough to settle the matter without additional witnesses."

I hadn't realized that while the officer was talking, several more people had joined us. Three police officers, a pair of EMTs, and a four-person crime scene unit all appear around us as we try to comprehend what has happened.

The whole time, Ben never lets go of my hand.

thirty-eight

I HAVE SCARS. Ben does too—mine are unflattering and show when I wear anything sleeveless, but Ben's are badass. I think he's proud of them.

After the night in Shreveport, we both ended up right back in the same hospital we'd worked so hard to escape from. Ben needed surgery to remove a splinter of broken rib from his lung, but the nurses said he'd be just fine, and they let us share a room while we both were treated. I was released after two days with a prescription for pain medication and bandages everywhere. Ben stayed in for almost a week.

At first, I think we both worried a little that without the loop pulling us together, we'd drift apart. The loop drew us to one another so we could *die* together, not necessarily so we could *live* together, and maybe without that special kind of gravity, we'd be just another couple. Maybe not even a couple at all.

But it didn't take long for us to realize it wasn't the loop that made us love each other. It was simply who we *are* that made us fall in love, and that's what keeps us together, too.

Ben wants to get a job somewhere in the Quarter this summer. He doesn't really seem to care where or what kind of work it is—busing tables or parking cars—as long as he's in the neighborhood he loves and has some money in his pocket so we can go out at night.

Springtime in Jackson Square is beautiful. Everything that can possibly bloom does. The grass is at its greenest, and a cool breeze rolls off the river. Restaurants open early for the lunch rush, and the smell of sautéed onions and peppers drifts through the open windows and doors of the cafés that surround the square. A brass band plays in front of the Saint Louis Cathedral.

Ben and I hold hands as we stroll past the tarot readers and artists, and weave through the tourists, who eye each neon-splattered canvas as though it were the *Mona Lisa.*

As usual, we're looking for Steve. Ben thinks Steve would really have his mind blown to see how we turned out, and we both want to thank him. We wouldn't be here today without his help.

It's been almost a year since we've seen him last. But every time we're in the Quarter, we still stop by his old corner of Jackson Square just in case he's there. And whenever we reach the spot where his table should be, instead of the familiar umbrella and Igloo cooler, there's always someone else. Today it's a man playing Spanish guitar. We put two bucks in his guitar case.

"I wonder where he is right now," Ben says. "I don't mean *now*, but . . . you know. In his own loop. If he's talking with us about Roy, or trying to explain to me how time is like a river. Or maybe he figured his way out of it by now."

"Maybe he's watching that marriage proposal he said he never misses."

Ben opens his mouth to speak, but stays silent. His gaze is fixed far across the square.

"What?" I ask. "You can say it."

"Maggie, do you think . . ." He hesitates before starting again. "I mean, do you think someday that could be us? You know, marriage and everything?"

He's sheepish and adorable. "Don't get ahead of yourself, Romeo."

"I thought we weren't Romeo and Juliet now," he says.

"I guess you're right—we're not really star-crossed lovers anymore, are we?"

"Well, not the star-crossed part," Ben says with a smile. "Still lovers, though."

I reply with a kiss—a soft one on his cheek. I slip my hand into his and let him lead me across Jackson Square to watch dusk settle over the river.

As we near Café Du Monde, I get the strangest sense of déjà vu.

acknowledgments

IT'S AMAZING just how many people are involved in publishing a book; you probably wouldn't believe me if I told you. I'm afraid of leaving someone out, so rather than list everyone individually, I'm just going to say thank you to my agent, John Rudolph, my editor, Emily Meehan, and her right hand, Laura Schreiber. Those three put far more work into this story than any writer would have a right to expect.

And then there is the army of family, friends, writers, and Other Random Motivators, all of whom deserve to be at the top of the list and none of whom should be relegated to the bottom. So, I'm going to be a chicken and not make a list. But I do hope you know who you are. Thank you.